Anna Wilson

Kitten Kaboodle

Illustrated by MOIRA MUNRO

MACMILLAN CHILDREN'S BOOKS

First published 2009 by Macmillan Children's Books
a division of Macmillan Publishers Limited
20 New Wharf Road, London N1 9RR
Basingstoke and Oxford
Associated companies throughout the world
www.panmacmillan.com

ISBN 978-0-330-50771-4

1 3 5 7 9 8 6 4 2

A CIP catalogue record for this book is available from
the British Library.

Typeset by Nigel Hazle
Printed and bound in the UK by CPI Mackays, Chatham ME5 8TD

In memory of my
lovely grandma Joan Davies,
who passed away while I was
writing this book.
We all miss you, Grandma.

1

My Petless State

My name is Bertie. And no, I'm not a boy. The name I was given when I was born was Roberta, but that stinks, so as soon as I had a say in the matter, I changed it to Bertie. So now you know.

Dad's name is Nigel Fletcher. He doesn't like his name much either, so when he does his job as a journalist (which he hates almost as much as his name), he signs his articles Marvin Fletcher instead. I don't much care what he calls himself, as I call him Dad, so it makes no difference to me.

For as long as I can remember it's been just the two of us, and life can get a bit lonely sometimes. This is the main reason why I started asking Dad very nicely from quite a young age if I could have a pet. That and the fact that I am, and always have been – and probably always will be – completely animal-mad. Dad has never shared my enthusiasm though, and also didn't seem to think I asked him nicely enough about having a pet, as his answer was always, 'Will you stop pestering me!'

His main reason for saying this was because he was a very busy man, as he was frequently telling me.

'I am a very busy man, you know, Bertie. I have to work hard and look after you.'

And he never got any help from anybody.

'And I don't get any help from anybody, so how the Dickens you think I've got room in my life for a pet, I don't know.'

Except I wasn't trying to get HIM to have a pet . . . it would be MY pet.

My Petless State

So I tried all kinds of different tactics to get him to see my point of view.

'Dad, what about a goldfish? They're easy pets to keep! And if I had a goldfish, it could sit on my desk and keep me company when I was doing my homework.'

'Bertie, a goldfish is the stupidest creature alive,' was Dad's rather random reply.

Honestly, did Dad really think I was going to *ask the goldfish* to help me with my maths and English and stuff? Also, it was rather a rude thing to say about goldfish. How did he know they were stupid, after all? Had he ever tried talking to one? They probably knew a whole lot more about swimming underwater than he did, not to mention blowing bubbles and keeping their eyes open without blinking.

OK. So . . . what about a budgie?

'They're small and cute and—'

'Bird flu,' said Dad. He wouldn't say any more

on the subject, clearly thinking that those two words said it all, which they didn't, as how can all budgies in the world have bird flu? They would all be dead and there would be no more budgies, which plainly isn't the case, or else the pet shop wouldn't still be selling them.

'A rabbit?' I tried again. 'They live off grass and the odd lettuce leaf or carrot, so they're not expensive, and they don't make any noise.'

'And who's going to clean it out?' Dad replied, crossing his arms and staring at me triumphantly.

'I will!' I said, crossing my arms and staring back triumphantly.

'You will not!' Dad said, snorting and uncrossing his arms. 'You can't even make your own bed.'

Another daft reply. Making my bed is a lot harder than sweeping up a few bits of straw and putting another few bits of straw into a hutch. My bed is on a platform and too high for me to reach

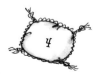
4

to tidy it properly, unless I am in it. But then once it is tidy I have to climb out of it, and that untidies it again. It is a definite no-win situation. So I don't bother any more. In any case, I don't poo in my bed like a rabbit does, so my bed doesn't need cleaning out in the same way.

'A dog?' I suggested, I admit quite quietly, as I already knew what the answer to that idea would be.

'A *WHAT*? ARE YOU CRAZY AND OUT OF YOUR MIND?'

So it would seem.

I tried the reasonable and logical approach. 'It's a great pet to have if you want to get fit, because you have to—'

'WALK IT EVERY DAY!!! WHICH IS WHY IT'S THE MOST RIDICULOUS IDEA I HAVE EVER—'

So the reasonable and logical approach wasn't going to work either. This was when I gave up.

Kitten Kaboodle

I could have carried on. I could have listed all the things which I knew would be the merits of having pet mice, or guinea pigs, or hamsters, or – a cat. But I already knew all the answers that would get thrown right in my face, and I was a bit fed up with all these conversations that ended in ends that were as dead as a dormouse. Or is that a doornail? (My animal obsession gets worryingly over-obsessive at times.)

If only Dad would chill out a bit, I thought. But Dad was not a chilling-out sort of person. He got stressed about everything, mainly his job, which he hated. As I said, he was a journalist; he worked for the local paper, the *Daily Ranter*. 'A journalist!' I hear you say. 'What an exciting job!'

Not. Dad was the kind of journalist who got sent to cover stories that would make you want to chew your arm off with boredom.

'Who in their right mind wants to read about

6

how appalling it is that the Christmas decorations have gone up too early, or what Mrs Miggles in the Post Office thinks about the new rubbish bins?' he would grumble. And he had a point.

But there was nothing I could do about Dad's job. And for as long as Dad was stressed out all the time, I could see that I was not going to be able to persuade him to let me have a pet. So I started looking out for opportunities to make friends with any animals I might come across in my day-to-day existence, without actually having to own one and have it live in the house.

Not much of a challenge, then.

First of all I tried looking around the garden to see if there were any friendly sparrows or blackbirds that I could get to know. I bought some bird-feeders with the last of my birthday money and hung them up in the trees to see if I could tempt any birds.

The feeders did tempt something, but it wasn't

1

a bird. It was a squirrel, and a rather vicious, fat one at that. The first time I saw it, I thought it looked quite cute and cuddly, so I moved a bit nearer.

'Hello!' I said quietly. 'You're a lovely little thing— OW!'

The nasty nut-nibbler chucked a peanut at me and hit me on the head! It was becoming clear that the garden was not going to be the place to offer me a pet, unless I was desperate enough to collect bugs and creepy-crawlies, which I was not. There is not much in the way of a relationship that you can develop with a beetle.

So I turned my attention to my general neighbourhood. There was a particularly lovely-looking kitten that had recently appeared around the place. I spotted him trotting up and down the pavement opposite our house and wondered who he belonged to. He was mostly black, but he had this stripe of white all along his tummy and right up his neck so it looked as if he was wearing one of those

posh dinner jackets with a white shirt on underneath. The posh look was rather spoilt, though, by the black splodge on his white nose and mouth that made him look as though he'd fallen face-first into a pot of ink. I liked that splodge best of all.

Once or twice I tried to get near enough to stroke him. I was desperate to touch that fluffy coat. But he froze for a split second when he saw me approach and I could have sworn he looked me up and down as if he were trying to decide whether or not he wanted to get to know me, and then he scarpered as if he'd decided he definitely didn't. I must have looked like a giant to him. It made me sad though, him running off like that. All I wanted to do was stroke him and hear him purr.

I was seriously beginning to despair of ever getting near an animal, forget the idea of actually owning one.

Then, one weekend when Dad was in his study writing all the time, I descended into an all-time record low of Boredom and Loneliness. I'd already done all my homework and tidied my room and packed my bag ready for school on Monday morning. I'd phoned round to find someone to hang out with, but everyone was busy.

'This is rubbish,' I told myself after I'd chewed off my last nail in sheer despair. 'You can't sit here all weekend and feel sorry for yourself.' So that was when I decided that I had to come up with a plan.

I got out a pad of paper and started brainstorming. It's what Dad does when he's got to write yet another article about a granny getting locked in the loos in the park and he can't think of how to spice it up. He gets a piece of paper and writes down all the words to do with the story and then draws arrows between the words to try and join them up in a fun way. He says, 'It helps to get the creative juices flowing.'

So I wrote down:

My Petless State

Dogs
Cats
Food
Walks
Owners
Hamsters
Feeding time
At home
Sausages
Hard work

Love
Cleaning out
Pets
Care for
Cages
Cuddles
Money
Guinea Pig
Liquorice

Those were some of the words that had come up in conversations with Dad about having a pet. They were also the first words that came into my head, which is why random things like 'sausages' and 'liquorice' got in there. But it doesn't matter that they were random. That's what brainstorming is all about, Dad says, as you never quite know what is going to lead where.

I started drawing lines between the words in a lazy, dreamy way, hoping that I would come up with a sentence which would jump off the page and give me a brilliant idea about how to solve my petlessness and general boredom with life.

Nothing happened to start with. All I got was:

Cats care for liquorice at home.

(Not true on any level, surely?)

And:

Dogs love hamster cuddles.

(More like 'Dogs love hamster-*burgers*.')

And:

Guinea pig walks cleaning out sausages.

(Weirderer and weirderer!)

The only thing these sentences made me do was giggle, which did cheer me up a bit, but didn't solve my problems of petlessness. 'One more try,' I

told myself, and half-heartedly picked up my pen again and joined up these words:

Care home for owners pets at.

I stared at it for a bit. But then I puffed out my cheeks and slumped back in my chair.

'Aaargh! None of this is making sense or helping me in any way,' I said, and my frustration made me screw up my face and screw up the paper at the same time and throw it across the room (the paper, not my face).

'What are you up to?'

Dad had come into the room. I do wish he would knock instead of just barging in on me like that. It's not that my life is so riveting that I am ever up to anything particularly private, but I have to knock on *his* study door when he's working, so you would think he could do the same for me. But as is often the case with grown-ups, it is one rule for him and one for me.

'Nothing,' I said, looking up at him through my eyebrows in a way that I hope said, 'None of your business!' without me actually having to be rude out loud.

'Oh. I just thought I heard you shout,' he said, looking puzzled.

'Well, I didn't,' I said, looking away from him and out of the window, which I vaguely noticed was a bit smeary from where I had squashed my nose up against it, trying to look around the corner to my best friend Jazz's house.

OK, so maybe I'm not as entirely lonely as I've been making out, but the thing is, Jazz has a big family and a busy life, so although she really is my best mate, she's not always on hand just when I need her. Her real name is Jasmeena, incidentally, which stinks almost as much as Roberta according to her, although I actually would prefer to be called Jasmeena than Roberta, but isn't that always the way? She lives in the same street as me, but it's

a bendy sort of street, so I can't really see her place from my window. I have always thought this was a shame, as I would love to be able to use those semaphore flags or the Morse code to communicate with her from my window. I know I can just pick up the phone or even go round there to see if she's free, but it's not as exciting. And I can't do those things in the dead of night anyway, as Dad would hear me and have a fit. (He has ears like an elephant and would definitely even hear something as quiet as semaphore flags waving. Come to think of it, I guess semaphore doesn't work in the dark—)

'Bertie?' Dad cut into my snake-like ramblings, jerking me back to reality.

'Still here then?' I muttered.

Dad inhaled deeply and said, 'So – what *are* you up to?'

I crossed my arms and held them tight around me. Could he not tell from my body language that I was not in the mood to be interrogated as if I were a criminal mastermind who had committed the most horrendous murder of all time? But then I realized that what Jazz always says was probably true: boys (and that presumably includes dads) don't understand body language.

Too late to do anything about it, I realized that Dad was stooping to pick up the piece of paper that I had thrown across the room.

'What's this?' he asked, un-scrunching it and smoothing it flat so that he could read it.

I panicked. 'Oh, er – I was just doing a bit of that creative brainstorming stuff that you do,' I blustered. I wished I could fade, chameleon-like, into the wallpaper and not have to face what was going to come next . . .

But Dad's mouth opened out into a huge grin and his eyes went sparkly.

'Hey, that's great, Bertie!' he said, crouching down to give me a half-hug. 'So what's your story going to be about then? Let's see what you've

written . . . "Care home for owners pets at"? Erm, doesn't make a lot of sense – unless that "at" isn't supposed to be there? "Care home for owners pets" – is that what you meant? There's an apostrophe missing there, you know. And a full stop.' He reached for the stubby pencil which seemed to live permanently behind his ear and made a mark on the scrunchy paper.

'Dad!' I was about to snatch the pencil out of his hand and snap back, 'I don't give a monkey's about apostrophes,' or possibly something ruder, when I realized what Dad had just done.

The previously nonsensical sentence,

Care home for owners pets at

had just become:

Care home for owners' pets.

OK, so that still sounded a bit weird – as if a load of old granny dogs were sitting in armchairs with blankets over their knees watching telly together, but nevertheless something had clicked inside my head and my brain suddenly felt well and truly stormed!

'Care for pets at owners' home!' I cried, then immediately realized what I'd said and clamped my hand over my mouth.

'Ye-es,' Dad said, frowning and nodding vaguely. He rubbed his hands though his hair and turned to walk out of the room. 'Well, I'll leave you to it, then. Got my own story to get on with. Yours sounds like it might be interesting . . .'

If only he'd known how right he was. With two tiny dots of his pencil and a bit of ultra-speedy brainstorming from yours truly, a great idea had been born.

I smiled secretively and hugged myself, whispering, 'Look out, world. Bertie Fletcher's Pet-Sitting Service is open for business.'

2
Business Woman of the Year

It was a complete brainwave of utter genius-ness, although I say it myself. People always had pets that they didn't have time to look after. It was a fact of modern hectic life — I was always readi-ng things like that in the *Daily Ranter*. In fact, there were frequently scaremongering stories about people who went on holiday and left their poor dog/cat/rabbit/gerbil home alone with no food and so on. Obviously people like that were monsters and deser-ved to have the RSPCA take their pets from them and make sure they could never in their lives ever again have the priceless privilege of being pet owners.

(Life was so unfair. Why were there people in the world with pets who could not even be bothered to look after them, and then there were people like me who weren't ALLOWED pets but who, if they *did* have them, would look after them *so* well they would live as royally as if they belonged to the Queen?)

This was where my brainwave came in (admittedly helped by Dad's apostrophe and full stop and general mega-grammar-fussiness, although I would never have told him that).

I, Bertie Fletcher, Pet-Sitter to the Stars (well, OK, our neighbours), would go to other people's houses and walk their dogs, or feed their cats or rabbits or whatever else they had – although I might possibly draw the line at stick insects or piranhas – and Dad would never have to know because the animals would stay in their owners' homes! I could just go round and feed them where they lived, right

there on the spot, without a single animal ever having to cross our threshold – Dad would never have to see an actual animal in his house ever.

I was so chuffed with my brainwave idea, that I immediately made some little notices with my best pens in some lovely curly writing. I wanted them to stand out from the usual boring post that people get:

Bertie Fletcher

Pet Sitter

I will look after your pets while you are away or out at work.

Tel 07896 546783

Kitten Kaboodle

'Dad!' I yelled across to his study, where he was once again glued to his computer screen, tapping away and muttering to himself. 'I'm just going to the shop!'

Dad grunted something at me about buying milk. I grabbed my hoody and the notices and ran.

As I closed the door behind me, I couldn't help grinning like a cat who's eaten all the custard. It was so exciting just imagining all the animals I would be asked to look after! I reminded myself to keep my mobile charged all the time, and I decided I should buy a nice diary to keep my appointments in. I was determined to be professional.

Of course I had not remembered that life doesn't often go the way you think it will. It's a fact I often forget about when I get excited.

I posted all the leaflets in every house in my street and on the way I spotted so many animals

that it made my tummy squirm just thinking about which ones I might be asked to help out with.

There was a house on the corner of the street that had two cute little King Charles spaniels with the hugest eyes I have ever seen on a real live creature that is not a cartoon. Mr Bruce who lived there was always out at work, and I knew that he often moaned to Dad about how expensive the dogwalker was, so I thought maybe he might be interested in my pet-sitting idea. I would not be expensive at all.

I could see the spaniels through the letterbox, jumping up at me when I put my leaflet through. There was quite a kerfuffly noise when the paper went through the door, a bit like something being scrunched or ripped. I chuckled as I thought about those naughty little dogs and wondered what they would be like to play with. They were yapping and yelping as I went back down the path, and I even wondered in a silly daydreamy kind of way if they had been able to read my notice and were looking forward to meeting me!

There were about forty houses in our street, which is a cul-de-sac. That means you can't get out the other end of it in a car – or a motorbike, or a camper van. You get the idea. The houses go round in a curve and sort of look out on to each other. Dad didn't like it. He said that everyone knew each other's business because it was like living in a goldfish bowl. Personally I didn't think it looked anything like a goldfish bowl, which is round and made of glass and full of water, whereas our street was very definitely dry and made of tarmac the last time I looked. And I thought it was cool as it meant we knew who nearly all of our neighbours were and people actually talked to each other, and of course one of those people was my best friend, Jazz. The other great thing about our road was that Dad let me go out on my own, as long as I stayed in the cul-de-sac and didn't try and escape into – shock, horror! – another street. (Anyone would think that the road next to ours was enemy territory or part of the Amazon rainforest or something.) But although I knew most people to say 'hello' to, one thing I wasn't one hundred per cent clear about was what kind of pets everyone had. For example, you know if someone has a dog because you see them (or a dogwalker) out walking with it, and you know when someone has a cat, as cats wander around all over the place. But you don't necessarily know if someone has a hamster or a goldfish or even a guinea pig unless you have been right inside their house or garden.

After all, it has been known for people to keep chinchillas or budgies in their bedrooms.

I suddenly had a moment of panic – as I was walking up the drive to Mr Sauna's house. He was a very quiet man who only ever said 'Good morning' or 'Good afternoon' or 'Good evening' and never anything else. Dad said it was because he was

Swedish and that his English was not that good. I had no idea what was in his house. What if he kept a ten-foot python in the garage and thought it would be a good idea to ask me to feed it for him while he was on holiday? I decided not to put a notice through his door.

Finally I came to number 15, which is over the road from our house. The person who lived in this house hadn't lived there long – only a couple of months – but Jazz and I had already decided from first sight that we didn't much like her. I know that is not fair, but 'Life is not fair', as Dad is fond of saying, and anyway lots of people judge by first appearances, even though they are probably the sort of people who will advise you not to.

Anyway, back to the lady at number 15. She was an actor, according to Dad, although I'd never seen her in any films or telly programmes, and her name was Fenella Pinkington. There, you see, even her name makes you want to not like her. In my

head (and when I was chatting to Jazz) I called her Pinkella, because she was always dressed from top to toe in pink, which is definitely *not* one of my favourite colours – all different kinds of shades of it, from very bright bubblegum pink through to soft pastelly, babyish pink. She was also embarrassing to talk to because the few times I'd spoken to her, she had insisted on calling me Roberta or, even worse, 'sweetie', *and* she touched my hair and told me in capital letters that it was 'DIVINE', which I did not like at all.

My hair is sort of darkish blonde and very, very curly. Ringlets is what Dad calls them. I don't mind it; I quite like it. It's not the sort of hair you *can* mind really, as it has a life of its own, so there is no point. What I *do* mind though is people touching it without asking. Especially if they use the words 'DIVINE' and 'sweetie' at the same time. How would Pinkella like it if I touched her pink floaty dresses? I wondered. But that was not a thought

27

Kitten Kaboodle

I wanted to hold on to for long, as those dresses looked decidedly nylony and itchy and would probably give me static electric hair, which with my ringlets would be nothing short of disastrous, if you think about it.

So the long and the short of it was that I almost didn't put a notice through Pinkella's door, but then I saw a kitten looking at me from the sitting-room window, where it was balancing on the sill. A kitten with a very distinctive dinner-jacket-with-cute-ink-splodge look.

Now, everyone knows that kittens are cute. But this kitten was *seriously* cute. It wasn't because he was at the really tiny, fluff-ball stage – he was older than that. He was into the long-legged, skinny, bouncy stage. I had seen him leaping and bounding around the street only the day before, batting his front paws (which were

white, like little boots on the end of his long black legs) at a bee in a very determined sort of way. His fur was silky shiny and he had bright yellow eyes that were still too big for his slim little baby-face. Maybe it was the eyes that did it for me. They were just so big. So golden.

I looked at him quite carefully, and in those yellow eyes there was a definite look that seemed to be trying to tell me something. I felt a shiver run up my spine. It was a sparkly kind of shiver that made me feel as though I was on the brink of something exciting.

I think that shiver was what made me put a notice through the door. Whatever it was, there was definitely a voice inside me saying that I should get to know that kitten better – even if it did mean having to put up with Pinkella patting my hair and calling me Roberta.

The more I thought about it, the more I realized that I could be quite a good business woman.

29

In fact, I could have gone on that programme on the telly called *In the Line of Fire,* where you have to present a new idea for a business and if you are good the man with the grey hair and the face like an angry potato says, 'You're hired!' and if you are rubbish, he says, 'You're fired!'

Maybe if I entered my pet-sitting idea on the programme I could get on it, I thought. It would be fun even if I was fired, as then I could say, 'Well, who cares? Your face looks like an angry potato.' It would give me a lot of satisfaction, actually.

One of the things that made me excited about the Pet-Sitting Service was that it would mean I would get some calls on my mobile, which I was now keeping glued to my side at all times. I had not received any calls for a long time as I had not been allowed to *make* any calls myself for over a year. This was all because of the incident with the first phone bill. Apparently I had spent enough money chatting to Jazz to feed a family of five for a month – Dad's words, not mine, in case you hadn't guessed. So I was only allowed to use it for emergencies from then on, such as if I was going to be coming out of school late or if Dad needed to tell me that he would be late back from work. But after the incident with the phone bill I was not allowed to use it to call my friends (especially Jazz) or text anyone. And seeing as Dad had never once called me on it and I had never once called him, I hadn't really seen the point in having it up until now.

As soon as Jazz had been released from her many weekend commitments (ballet followed by tap followed by piano followed by singing – you'd never have guessed she wants to be a celebrity pop-star-singer-songwriter when she grows up, would you?) I went round to hers to tell her everything.

'It's *such* a cool idea, Bert!' she said, hugging me

and jumping up and down, which made my face squish uncomfortably into the zip on her hoody.

'Yeah,' I said, prising her off. 'You want to help?'

'You bet!' Jazz cried, punching the air and swivelling round on the spot in one of her so-called funky dance moves. 'Sooo, who d'you reckon will call first? I hope it's that lady with the guinea pigs. I loooove guinea pigs!' she squealed, sounding a bit like one herself.

'Which lady with the guinea pigs?' I asked, feeling a bit miffed that I had not known about a lady with guinea pigs in our street. But Jazz wasn't listening – she was whirling round her room, jabbering away about all the animals we'd soon be looking after and how much money we'd be making.

I kept glancing at my phone, which I'd put on Jazz's bed so that I would hear it clearly when it rang. It was bound to ring soon, wasn't it? Of

course it was, I told myself. In fact, now that I was on course for being Pet-Sitter and Business Woman of the Year, my phone was going to be ringing so much I might actually have to buy *another* one to keep up with the demand.

3

Call Number One

Three whole days went by and no one called. I was jittery with nerves. So was Jazz, which made me even more jittery as she kept asking, 'You will tell me the *moment* someone calls, won't you?'

Every time the house phone rang I jumped, thinking it was my mobile. This shows just how agonizingly jittery I really was, as the two phones do not sound remotely the same: my phone has a weird ringtone on it that Jazz recorded, which is her voice shout-ing, *Yay, Bertie! Yay, Bertie!* like some kind of manic American cheerleader. (She did it for a

Yay, Bertie! Yay, Bertie!

laugh one break time. I don't know how to get rid of it, and Jazz won't get rid of it for me.)

'It was such a lame plan in the first place,' I said to Jazz on Day Three, slumping into her purple beanbag with the stars on. 'I don't know why I thought I could change my life overnight with some stupid babyish pet-sitting idea.'

'Hey, don't get stressy!' Jazz said, sounding, if I may be so bold, quite stressy herself. 'Maybe the neighbours haven't gone through their post yet. We get so many pizza leaflets and stuff. Mum just chucks them all on the side and goes through everything at the weekend.'

'Oh, huge amounts of thanks for your un-dying support, dear friend,' I said sarcastically. 'So my leaflet is like junk mail, you mean?'

Jazz ignored me and carried on pacing up and down her room, ticking off possible reasons for our neighbours' non-communicativeness. 'Or maybe no one needs a pet-sitter right now. It's not the holidays yet. Maybe they've pinned your notice up and they'll call you when they need you.'

I huffed and puffed and took out all my grumpiness on Jazz, which was unfair, but luckily for our friendship Jazz is pretty good at putting up with my moods (i.e. ignoring them), and double-luckily I didn't have to keep up the grumpiness for long as someone finally called the next afternoon.

Unfortunately it was at a very inconvenient time and completely took me by surprise. This was mainly because it was the one day when Dad had actually offered to pick me up from school rather than making me take the bus.

Yay, Bertie!
Yay, Bertie!

Call Number One

'What the—?' Dad leaped about a mile and a half out of his seat and the car lurched dangerously to the right, causing the traffic coming in the other direction to swerve and honk noisily at us. A man leaned out of his car window and shouted and made a sign with his hand that was definitely not a friendly kind of sign.

'It's just my phone,' I said, rummaging in my bag and trying to push down the excited and fluttery feelings in my tummy and smother them with a layer of calmness instead.

'Your *what*?' Dad snapped, glaring at me in the rear-view mirror.

'My phone – you know, that extremely modern invention which allows humankind to converse with other members of the species from a distance while— I'd better answer it,' I said hastily and not at all calmly. 'Hello?'

'Hello, sweetie!'

I froze.

37

'Hello?' the voice continued. 'That is Roberta Fletcher, isn't it?

No, it's BERTIE Fletcher, I screamed inside my head, all tangled up with panic and annoyance and confusion.

'It's Fenella Pinkington, your neighbour from over the road?'

I'd kind of guessed that, SWEETIE. Why on earth was *she* calling?

'I'm ringing in response to your imaginative business idea . . .' She paused. 'The Pet-Sitting Service?'

Of course – the kitten! My tummy clenched itself into a ball as tight and spiky as a baby hedgehog.

'Ye-es?' I said hesitantly.

'Well, darling, I was wondering if you might like to come and meet my little kitty-cat.' Pinkella wittered on in my ear while I was quietly freaking in my seat. How was I going to talk about my

Call Number One

Pet-Sitting Service right that instant with Dad listening in?

'I was wondering if you'd be free—' Pinkella continued.

'Oh, right, sorry. Wrong number,' I said quickly, and cut her off.

Darnation and hell-busters! I was in a right state. Why did she have to call while I was in the car with Dad? This was my one and only call from a true and genuine client wanting my Pet-Sitting Services, and I'd just gone and put the phone down on her! Even if it was Pinkella Deville, I still wanted her custom – especially since she was the only person to bother replying to my advert and double-especially since she was the owner of that seriously cute, ink-splodge-to-die-for kitten.

'Bit odd, you getting a call,' said Dad, glancing at me in the mirror again, his eyebrows raised in a suspicious expression.

'Hmm,' I said, in a non-committal way, looking out of the window.

'Why have you even got your phone on anyway? I'm the only person with the number and I'm right here. You should turn it off to save the batteries. Unless . . . You and Jazz haven't been calling each other again, have you? What on earth have you two got to talk about that's so important you need to call each other every moment of every day? You're in school together the whole time, for heaven's sake. I bet you've been texting too. It'll cost a fortune! You know that phone is only for emergencies.'

I slouched in my seat and rolled my eyes. (No wonder he worked on the *Daily Ranter*, I thought. He *was* the daily ranter. No, make that the *hourly* ranter.)

'Yes, Dad,' I said wearily. 'I mean, no, Dad. I mean . . .'

I was not really listening to him as I was sur-

reptitiously saving Pinkella's number so that I could call her back later. Meanwhile my brain continued whirring into a head-spin. What would I say? I had been quite rude, cutting her off like that.

I know! I had a flash of inspiration. I'd tell Pinkella it was *Jazz* who had answered the call because she had taken my phone home instead of hers by mistake.

Dad parked the car, and I scuttled inside and up to my bedroom for some privacy.

'Don't you want a snack?' Dad called after me.

'In a minute – need the loo!' I called back, and veered into the bathroom to put Dad off my scent. I needn't have worried though – Dad was already disappearing into his study to get on with yet more work.

But for once, I didn't care.

I shut the bathroom door and locked it just in case and then sat down on the edge of the bath. I took a deep breath and then turned my phone back on. I called up Pinkella's number on my screen and pressed the green dial button. She answered on the second ring.

'Hello?'

'Er, yes, hello – erm, it's Bertie Fletcher.'

'Oh, hello, Roberta,' said Pinkella, sounding puzzled. 'That's funny. I tried ringing you a few minutes ago and the person who answered told me I'd got the wrong number.'

'Ye-es,' I faltered. 'That was my, er, my assistant, er, Jasmeena.' I used her full name as it sounded more serious than 'Jazz'. 'Well, she's more of a friend than an assistant, but she assists me, you see,' I warbled, wincing and thinking what an utter nut-brain I sounded.

'Oh dear, sweetie! If you take my advice, you'll get yourself a new assistant – one who knows a thing or two about assisting! Heeeheeeheee!' she twittered in that tinkling titter of hers. Even her voice sounds pink, I thought.

Call Number One

'Yes, I – I'm thinking of doing just that,' I said, feeling a bit of confidence return, and putting on the most professional voice I could under the circumstances. 'So, how can I help you, Pin— Ms Pinkington? I hear that you received one of my leaflets?' I hoped my more businesslike tone would stop her from thinking I was actually a bonkers person who could not be trusted with looking after a used tea bag, let alone her beloved cat.

'Please, call me Fenella, sweetie,' she tinkled. 'Yes, I was simply *thrilled* to get your leaflet – it came absolutely in the nick of time. You see, I'm due to go away for a couple of weeks and I was starting to get into a teensy bit of a panic about poor little Kaboodle here. Isn't that right, Kaboodle?'

At that point I heard a very loud purring noise right in my ear. I nearly dropped the phone.

'There! Did you hear that, sweetie? Kaboodle

agrees with me!' said the worryingly insane woman on the other end of the phone. 'You see,' she continued, as I shook my head sadly, 'my previous cat, Pusskins, God rest his soul, used to have a room at the gorgeous cat hotel in town – do you know it?' She broke off to blow her nose.

Oh no. She's going to start blubbing down the phone about her old dead cat, I panicked. 'Er, no, no I don't,' I said, hastily adding, 'but I'm sure it's lovely.'

'Yes,' sniffed Pinkella. '"Purrfect Heaven" it's called. It's just off the high street, behind that hairdresser's with the lovely fuchsia curtains. Of course, poor Pusskins has gone to the real purrfect heaven in the sky now . . . Anyway, I'm getting off the point,' she sighed and blew her nose again.

Were you ever on it? I wondered.

'I was *so* desperate for darling little Kaboodle here to go to the same cat hotel, where I *know* they would treat him most royally, but to my *utter*

despair, when I phoned them this morning, they told me they were fully booked! Well, I simply *cannot* cancel this trip. I'm auditioning for the leading role in a new romantic comedy by that gorgeous man Richard Elton – *Love, Don't You Know?*, I think they're calling it – and the auditions are in *Scotland* of all places.' She made a noise that sounded rather like a shudder. 'So,' she continued, 'how much do you charge?'

It took me a moment to realize that Pinkella had stopped wibbling and that she had asked me a question, and then it took me another moment to realize that she was offering me actual, real money.

'I – er . . .' I hadn't given one single thought to how much I would charge for this Pet-Sitting Service – what an idiot! Some Business Woman of the Year I was turning out to be. I could just see the angry potato man saying, 'YOU'RE FIRED!' in a booming voice, and it was not a picture that did much for my self-confidence or ability to think clearly under pressure.

'Erm – sort of a pound a day?' I said.

'My goodness, you do come cheap!' she trilled. 'Well, I think you'd better come round and be formally introduced to Kaboodle as soon as possible. He can't wait to meet you, can you, little kitty-kins?'

'I'll have to check with my dad,' I said, my head still spinning, even though I actually had no intention whatsoever of checking with Dad.

'Good girl,' said Pinkella. 'You can pop by any time. I'll be in – I've still not packed my suitcases yet and I must practise my lines. Toodle-oo!'

Toodle-what?

I said goodbye and pressed the red button on my phone.

'Yes, yes!' I cried, thumping the air, and doing a little victory dance. My first customer! I had to tell Jazz.

Call Number One

The doorbell rang, jolting me out of my cheery prancing. I jumped and dropped my phone, narrowly missing the loo.

'Ber-tie!' Dad was calling me.

I unlocked the bathroom door, opened it and peered out. 'Ye-es?' I said, feeling a bit sick. What if it was Pinkella, come round right away to talk to me in person?

'Are you still on the loo?' Dad yelled. This immediately made my sick feeling turn into a grumpy one. That man has made being an embarrassment into an Olympic sport, I thought.

'Hey, Bertie!'

Phew! That didn't sound like Pinkella.

'Jazz?' I said, coming down the stairs.

'Mum thought you might like to come round to ours for tea.'

'Yay! Dad – can I?' I looked at him with my most pleading face. This would solve all my problems at once! I could say I was going to Jazz's, but just pop in on Pinkella on the way. Plus I loved going for tea at Jazz's. It was so full-on and noisy, with her little brother, Tyson, zooming round the place making aeroplane noises and the rest of the family all talking at once. Quite a lot different from my silent-as-the-tomb-type house.

Dad didn't look as though he would even be able to say what day it was, let alone take much notice whose house I was at, I realized as I inspected his face. He had his Deadline Head on, which meant he had an article that needed to be handed in to the *Daily Ranter* very soon and it was stressing him out. Poor Dad. He looked terrible – as if he had not slept for more than about ten minutes all week. Why hadn't I noticed this when he picked me up from school? I thought guiltily. I had been too wrapped up in my own thoughts about pet-sitting and money-making. I chewed my lip.

His hair (which is curly like mine, although

there's not as much of it) was sticking up on end in a rather woolly sheep-type fashion, which is what it does when he runs his hands through it a lot, and his eyes had sunk further into his head than is normal for a human being. The skin around his eyes was also quite dark. Actually, he looked more like a slightly baffled owl than a sheep.

Come to think of it, I should have realized something was up that morning as he had drunk fifteen cups of coffee one after the other while muttering, 'What am I going to write? What am I going to write?' These are the usual signs that a deadline is on the horizon, or indeed is charging towards Dad from the horizon at about one hundred miles an hour.

'Sure. Be back by seven,' he said finally, distractedly running his hands through his hair.

'What's up?' said Jazz, as we closed the front door behind us. 'When I arrived you looked like you'd just won a year's supply of chocolate and now you look as if you wish you hadn't eaten it all in one go!'

'Oh, yeah. Just a bit worried about Dad,' I muttered. But I fixed a grin back on my face and said brightly, 'But listen. This is a zillion times more interesting!' I told her about Pinkella and Kaboodle.

'Kaboodle? What kind of weirdo name is that?' she said, curling her top lip in her you've-just-said-something-random expression.

'I know – not the coolest—' I agreed.

'And you didn't ask for a POUND a day, did you?' Jazz interrupted.

'Ye-es.'

'You doofus! A poxy pound a day! No wonder she wants you to look after her dear little pussy-cat. You should have said a fiver – *and* you should have asked for a deposit! Don't you know anything about business?'

'But I don't care about the money, Jazz!' I

exclaimed. 'Don't you get it? I'm finally going to have a pet to look after. I'm going to get to feed him and cuddle him and play with him! YAY!' I cried, dancing round and round.

'No need to be freaky about it,' said Jazz, but she was grinning. 'So can I be your *business partner* then?' she asked, putting on a posh voice.

'You can be my official assistant,' I said, hugging her. 'I told Pinkella I needed a new one.'

'Eh?'

'Never mind – come on, let's go round there now. Kitten-sitters R Us!'

4

Welcome to the House of Pink

You would have thought Jazz and I were celebrities the way Pinkella welcomed us.

'Roberta!' she cooed, opening her arms wide.

Please don't hug me, I cringed.

She hugged me. Tight. Urgh. My face was pressed into her pongy pinkness and I nearly gagged on her overpoweringly sick-making flowery perfume.

'Ro-*who*?' said Jazz.

I wriggled away as politely as it is possible to wriggle away from someone you don't know that well, and scowled at Jazz warningly.

Welcome to the House of Pink

'And the beautiful Jasmeena!' said Pinkella, reaching out and cupping Jazz's chin in her spiky, jewel-covered fingers. 'What gorgeous eyes you have, sweetie!'

It's true, Jazz does have gorgeous eyes. They're like those shiny chocolate drops in the sugar casing, and they're huge. She's got mega eyelashes too. If I didn't know better I'd say she had false ones, but they're not – her whole family's got them. I've always been really jealous of the way Jazz can use her chocolate-drop eyes to get pretty much whatever she wants from people.

It seemed she wasn't going to use them on Pinkella though: she scowled and her smooth brown cheeks darkened as she squirmed out of Pinkella's clutches. 'I prefer "Jazz",' she said sourly. 'So where is Noodle?'

Pinkella dissolved into fits of hysterics about nothing in particular, as far as I could see. 'Oooh!

You are cute! Follow me – I think *Kaboodle* is having a little nap on his cushion.'

Jazz raised her eyebrows at me, a definite sign that her already unenthusiastic opinion of Pinkella was not improving by the minute. She held up one hand to me and splayed out the fingers, mouthing, 'A fiver!'

I put a finger to my lips and frowned at her.

Pinkella came back out into the hall with a small soft bundle of gorgeous black and white fur. 'Here he is, the little *darling*,' she said, nuzzling her powdery face into the kitten's coat. 'You were sleeping, weren't you, my little koochy-koo? But you must wake up and meet these lovely girlies who are going to be looking after you while Mummsie is away.'

Kaboodle raised his small, neat head and stared at us, his ears alert and his yellow eyes widening into deep pools of cuteness. That shivery feeling overtook me again. It was almost like static elec-

tricity, like when you walk on a nylony carpet and then touch something metal; and once again I was absolutely convinced that Kaboodle was trying to tell me something. But what?

'Would you like to take him, Roberta sweetie?' Pinkella asked, holding him out to me.

I was really nervous now. What if I dropped him? What if looking after him was going to be a nightmare? What if—?

Pinkella softly dropped him into my hands, a tiny parcel of warm kittenness, purring fatly, pushing his head against my arm as if *he* was stroking *me*! That purr was such a warm, friendly sound. The shivery sensation settled down into a soft buzz and I let out the breath I'd been holding in. He liked me.

'Look at you!' said Jazz, pointing a chewed-off purple-painted fingernail at me and laughing. 'Don't go all soppy on me now!'

'Hisssss!' Kaboodle jerked his head away from

55

me and spat at Jazz. I was so freaked, I nearly dropped him.

'Now, now, Kaboodle darling,' cooed Pinkella. 'Don't be a naughty boy. These sweet little girls will look after you just like Mummsie does.'

I tentatively stroked Kaboodle's back to try and calm him down. The fur on the back of his neck had gone spiky and he felt tense and uncomfortable in my arms. 'Shh, it's all right,' I whispered in one flattened ear. 'I promise I'll take care of you.'

Jazz rolled her eyes and waggled her head at me, setting off the beads in her hair. 'You are too much!' she drawled. 'Chatting away to that little kitty-cat like he understands every word. You kill me!'

'Oh but he does understand, don't you, Kaboodle sweetie-pie?' said Pinkella. I would have joined in with Jazz and rolled my own eyes, but before I could say anything, Kaboodle twisted his head around to look up at me. And I was sure, absolutely positive, that he winked.

I gasped and flicked a glance at Jazz. Had she seen it too? But she was still laughing at me and shaking her head as if I was a complete nut-brain. Which I was beginning to think I was . . .

Imagine if I told Jazz that this adorable little cat had just winked at me! She would take one look at me and circle her finger round next to her brain and say, 'Tick-tock, tick-tock, curly-wurly CUCKOO!' or something equally intelligent and insightful.

Instead I forced a grin and said, 'Looks like he does understand me, Ms P!'

Pinkella beamed. 'Well, it certainly seems you two – sorry, three,' she added hastily, seeing the set expression on Jazz's face, 'are going to get along like a house on fire. Now, I hope you don't mind but I've drawn up a short list of things to remember while I'm away, and I've left the number of the hotel I'll be staying at too, just in case.'

Normally I hate it when grown-ups fuss like that. It's so annoying; it's like they think we can't handle things on our own even though we seem to manage OK – catching buses to and from school, doing our homework and getting to after-school clubs on time . . . This time, though, I *wasn't* listening. I was totally focused on the warmth in my arms, listening to Kaboodle purring and thinking: *this* is what I have been waiting for.

What if Pinkella is right and he *can* actually understand every word we say? I wondered dreamily, as Pinkella and Jazz wittered on to each other somewhere in the vague and cloudy distance. Wouldn't that be cool?

But then I realized it would all be a waste of time unless I developed the magic gift of being able to talk to animals, like that Doctor Dolittle guy I'd seen in a film once. I shook my head. I

would end up as bonkers as Pinkella if I wasn't careful.

I became dimly aware of Pinkella handing Jazz a piece of paper and saying, 'If you think I've missed anything, or there's anything you don't understand, please don't hesitate to call.'

'Oh, right, thanks,' I muttered, and reluctantly handed Kaboodle over to Pinkella, who was beaming at him with outstretched arms.

'That's right, come to Mummsie,' she crooned through puckered lips. 'Mummsie's got to get as many cuddles as she can before she has to leave poor little Kaboodle, hasn't she?'

Jazz shot me a look of utter contempt and said, 'Well, thanks, Ms P. I think we know what to do. There's just one small matter we have to discuss before we go, though.' She looked meaningfully at Pinkella with one eyebrow raised.

'What's that, sweetie?' Pinkella asked, still cooing over Kaboodle.

Jazz coughed and said, 'Er – we at Bertie Fletcher's Pet-Sitting Service always require a down payment before taking on any job—'

'Jazz!' I couldn't believe this.

But Jazz shook her head at me and frowned. 'It's like protection against you changing your mind or anything?' she added, putting a hand on one hip and rattling her bangles officiously.

Pinkella chewed her bottom lip. If I hadn't been so worried she was about to bawl us out for being cheeky, I would have said she was trying not to laugh.

'Of course, dear. How much did you say it was going to be?' she asked, looking at Jazz, not me, I noticed.

'Five—'

'A pound a day,' I said firmly, ignoring Jazz's fierce stare of disbelief.

'That's right, I remember now,' said Pinkella. She set Kaboodle down on a hideous bubblegum-

pink cushion and fiddled in an equally gross-coloured handbag for her purse. 'Here you are – I'll give you five pounds for now, and we'll settle up when I come back. How does that sound?'

'Great,' said Jazz, stepping in front of me and snapping up the money.

I rolled my eyes, but decided not to say anything.

'Now – one last question, Ms P.'

'Yes, Jasmeena?'

'What do we do if Kaboodle catches a mouse or something?' she asked, pulling the corners of her mouth down and giving an exaggerated shudder.

I flinched. I had not thought of that. Jazz was right – cats did that kind of thing all the time.

Pinkella looked appalled. 'Oh dearie me, Kaboodle is far too much of a little baby to do that sort of thing, aren't you, *darling*?' she asked, looking at her kitten who was now back on his silky pink cushion, washing his front paws very carefully. He

looked up as Pinkella spoke and blinked
slowly as if he was thinking about
what to say in response. 'There,
you see!' said Pinkella triumphantly. 'He says of course
he wouldn't!'

Jazz gave me a sideways
glance and pursed her lips.

I cleared my throat loudly and said, 'Well, that's
all right then,' and made a move towards the door.
'Have a good time in Scotland, Ms P!' I said cheer-
fully. I still couldn't bring myself to call her Fenella.
'Hope you get that part in the film.'

'Thank you, Roberta,' said Pinkella, beaming.
'I'll be back in a fortnight. And good luck with
Kaboodle – although I'm sure you won't need it.
He's such a well-behaved little boy.'

'Miiia-oow!' Kaboodle answered in a kittenish
mew.

Was he agreeing with her?

Welcome to the House of Pink

Jazz hardly waited until the door was shut on us before giving her verdict.

'That woman is a *serious* fruit-loop!' she crowed.

'Shut up!' I hissed nervously. 'She might hear you!' I glanced hastily over my shoulder to see if she was still standing in the doorway. But I needn't have worried. Pinkella was at the living-room window, Kaboodle held in a firm embrace, and – oh no, dear me, no . . .

'She's making him wave his ickle-wickle paw at us!' Jazz screamed hysterically, pointing at the insane scene in front of us.

I nodded and smiled stiffly at Pinkella and waved back at her and Kaboodle. 'Stop it, Jazz,' I said out of the corner of my forced grin. 'Just think of the money.'

Jazz grinned at me, pirouetted and did a snaky dance move with her arms, singing, 'Oh yeah!' and flourishing the five-pound note at me.

Kitten Kaboodle

I grinned back and then turned to take one last careful look at Kaboodle before heading to Jazz's house.

And that time, he definitely did wink. No doubt about it.

5

Gourmet Delights

Dad would have liked Pinkella's note. It was in the most beautiful handwriting; the letters were perfectly even with not a crossing-out in sight. They were also written in smart black fountain-pen ink, not scrabbly pencil or biro, which is what I would have used. Dad is always going on about how messy my writing is. 'Messy writing shows a messy mind,' he says. He also says that I need to 'Pay more Attention to Detail'. In fact, that's one of his favourite sayings. That and: 'Tone of Voice!'

Funnily enough, the way I tend to respond to being told to 'Pay Attention to Detail' often invites the comment 'Tone of Voice!' straightaway afterwards.

Anyway, Pinkella would win the Attention to Detail Award no problem, and not simply because of her handwriting. This was what she had written:

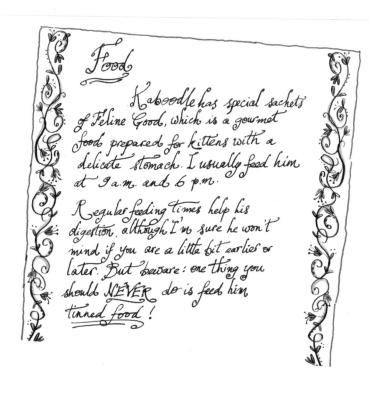

Food

Kaboodle has special sachets of Feline Good, which is a gourmet food prepared for kittens with a delicate stomach. I usually feed him at 9 a.m. and 6 p.m.

Regular feeding times help his digestion, although I'm sure he won't mind if you are a little bit earlier or later. But beware: one thing you should NEVER do is feed him tinned food!

Drink

Please use the filtered water in the fridge. Unfiltered tap water or milk gives Kaboodle tummy ache.

Cat Flap

Please check the cat flap regularly to make sure it is not stuck.

If Kaboodle cannot get in and out he may have a little accident, which embarrasses him terribly.

One final thing

Kaboodle is used to company. Please come round as often as you can to cuddle him.

Jazz whistled long and low after reading the note through and shook her head. 'That cat doesn't know he's born!' she said. 'I wish Mum treated *me* that well.'

'What – fancy the odd sachet of Feline Good, do you?' I teased.

Jazz pushed me sharply on the arm and squealed, 'GROSS!' And she started dancing round, singing out the song they use in the ad for Feline Good on the telly: '*Feline Good! Der-der-der-der-der-der-der! You know that it's good now! Feeeee-line Gooood!*'

'Put a sock in it, Jazz,' I grinned. 'It's bad enough on the ad, without your caterwauling version.'

She spun round and pointed at me, holding her other hand to her face as if it were a mike. 'Ha! Cat-erwauling! I like that, babe. Hey, you know what?' she said, dropping her hands and fixing me with a serious look. 'They do say that there are people in those pet food factories who actually have to *taste* the pet food before it goes to the shops?'

Gourmet Delights

'Urgh, Ja-azz!' I protested. 'Now who's being gross? That stuff stinks! There's no way in a million years that anyone would actually *taste* it.'

Jazz stuck her chin in the air and squared her shoulders. 'I don't know. I would – if the money was good enough,' she said.

'Now you are seriously freaking me out,' I said, horrified. 'Can we change the subject, please? We've got work to do.'

Jazz rolled her eyes and grinned. 'OK, OK. Whatever you say, boss. Let's get started on the Appointments Book.'

We were back at her house now and I had brought my new red ring-bound notebook with me. I was going to use it to write down everything I needed to remember about which animals I was pet-sitting.

'As your assistant I'll take care of writing down all the appointments for you!' Jazz said, bouncing on to one of her beanbags.

Kitten Kaboodle

Secretly I thought I could probably manage to write them down myself, but I just said, 'Cool. And I'll make some notes about what Kaboodle needs.'

'Hey, let's check out cats on the Web,' said Jazz, bouncing up from her beanbag and going over to her desk where her silver laptop was lying.

Jazz has a lot of stuff I don't, like a laptop and a TV in her room, and bunk beds. And a mum.

We searched for websites that might have top tips on how to look after cats, but we got a bit distracted by some pretty scary stories about the mad things that cats can get up to. And there were certainly more than a few tales about the kind of 'presents' that cats had brought their owners – like live frogs, for example.

'Urgh – gross!' Jazz cried. 'Lucky you don't have to *live* with Kaboodle. Imagine a live frog in your actual house!'

'Yeah, but Kaboodle doesn't catch anything yet, remember?' I told her.

Gourmet Delights

'Yeah, and I'm the Queen of Fairyland,' said Jazz. 'All cats catch stuff, Bertie. It's in their blood. Kaboodle might be a baby to Pinkella, but he's not a newborn kitten, is he? He's probably just really good at finishing off what he catches instead of leaving it for Pinkella to find.'

'Do you mind?' I protested. 'I'd rather not talk about it. It's disgusting. You're in a weird mood today, Jazz.' I thought about those round yellow eyes and shook my head. There was no way that little cat would cause me any trouble at all, I was convinced of it.

Pinkella left for Scotland early that Saturday. I was going to say 'bright and early', except it wasn't bright because I was up before the sun had peeped over the top of the houses in our street, and that's when I saw her leave. I was so excited about the idea of finally being a pet-owner – OK, a pet-sitter – that I hadn't been able to sleep properly. I saw Pinkella glance up at my window and give me a cheery wave as she got into her taxi. She was wearing a coat that went right down to the ground and was made entirely of pink fake fur (at least I hope it was fake – surely no real animal has bad enough taste to be that colour in real life?). She also had high-heeled dark pink shoes on. She certainly was a loony, but something told me she might actually be quite a nice loony.

I couldn't wait to go round and feed Kaboodle. I'd been agonizing about how I was going to be able to do it without arousing Dad's suspicion, as it was unlike me to be dressed on a Saturday before ten o'clock, let alone out of the house. I was usually watching telly, and there had to be a world event of universe-shattering proportions for me to agree to change out of my Snoopy PJs before lunchtime.

So the night before I had been about to ask him if I could go and help Jazz get Tyson dressed in the morning (bad excuse and totally unbeliev-able, I know, especially seeing as Ty is seven and

perfectly capable of getting dressed on his own – but I was desperate!). But then Dad saved me the trouble.

'I'm really sorry, Bertie, but I'm going to have to ask Jazz's mum if you can go round there early tomorrow. I know it's the weekend, but I've got to go out and do some research for this article I'm writing about a new multi-storey car park in the town. Apparently everyone's very upset because the plan is to knock down the old theatre and build the car park in its place.'

How thrilling – I didn't think. If ever Dad were to tell me he had high hopes of me following in his footsteps as a journalist, I would have to tell *him* that he was the 'Weakest Link. Goodbye.' I would rather eat a tonne of Brussels sprouts. Raw. With mustard.

'Sounds riveting,' I said, grinning cheekily. 'I'm sooooo disappointed you don't want me to come with you.'

Kitten Kaboodle

'No need to be sarky, young lady,' said Dad. 'So you don't mind going to Jazz's then?' he asked, peering at me in a very concerned manner as if he'd just discovered my homework was to recite all my tables backwards, instead of telling me to go to my best friend's house on a Saturday morning.

'Er, no, Dad. Funnily enough, I don't!'

So that is why at nine o'clock that Saturday I was not in my Snoopy PJs, but was fully dressed in my best dark denim skinnies with my favourite stripy top on, and a pink band in my hair, which I'd put on specially for the occasion so Kaboodle would feel at home with me. (Don't ask me where someone who hates pink gets a pink hairband from. I just found it in a drawer, OK?) I waited on Jazz's doorstep, pet-sitting appointments book and cat information pack in hand, all fired up and ready to go.

Jazz opened the door and threw her arms around me.

Gourmet Delights

'Happy Pet-Sitting Day!' she yelled, squeezing me tight and squashing her bangles into me.

THWACK! Tyson careered into Jazz's back and shrieked, 'Happy Poo-Sitting Day!' and giggled like a maniac.

'Ty – buzz off!' Jazz yelled. 'This is a girls' only moment. No brat brothers allowed.'

'Ty-son! Leave your sister alone!' Jazz's mum shouted down the hall and for once Ty did as he was told. Although not until he'd stuck his tongue out and blown a full-on raspberry for good measure.

'Idiot,' Jazz hissed.

'He's cute!' I said.

Jazz curled her lip at me. Then she gave me a quick once-over and smirked. 'Hey, like the pink hairband – Ms P would approve. So. How did you manage to get out so early?'

I shrugged. 'Didn't Dad tell your mum? He's got some ultra-boring meeting about a car park that used to be a theatre or something. Anyway, don't talk so loud – remember I don't want Dad to find out about the pet-sitting.'

'OK, OK, don't get stressy,' said Jazz, wobbling her head at me and putting on what Dad would definitely have called a Tone of Voice. 'Mum's dealing with Ty and everyone else is still snoring.'

We headed off, arm in arm.

'I've been thinking, Berts. We really need to look again at the business side of this enterprise,' Jazz said, her voice all bouncy and glittery.

'Eh?'

'The *money*, Bertie – you should be asking for more.'

I shook my head. 'No, I'm not going to. A pound a day for two weeks is already a lot of money. And we only have to go over there twice a day.'

'WHAT?' Jazz shrieked. 'What kind of a business woman are you? You've got to know the

market rate in any business transaction,' she added confidently, as if she actually knew what she was talking about.

'I'm not really interested in the money,' I said impatiently.

I regretted it the moment the words were out of my mouth.

'WHA—?' Jazz began again, her jaw dropping dramatically as if I had finally lost every last marble in my brain and she was watching them roll away at top speed into the nearest gutter.

'Listen,' I interrupted, stopping suddenly, which caused my whirling dervish friend to whirl dervishly into me. We disentangled ourselves. 'I've already told you – I don't care about the money because that's not why I set up the Pet-Sitting Service in the first place!' I said, putting a hand up to stop her from butting in, which is what she was about to do. 'You *know* I've always wanted a pet of my own. You *know* Dad won't let me. So you should understand that the only thing I want to get out of this idea of mine is a chance to look after some animals and – well, I know it sounds lame – kind of pretend that they are actually my own for a bit.'

Jazz's face changed when I said this. She smiled a small smile and dropped her head to one side. 'All right,' she said, putting her arm around me. 'Come on then, you noodle; let's go cuddle Kaboodle!'

6

Cat-astrophe!

In Pinkella's kitchen she'd left another note on the work surface in some more of that seriously classy handwriting. It was written on, you've guessed it, pink notepaper. And it honked of some of the overpoweringly flowery perfume Pinkella was wearing when she had tried to crush me to death.

Her signature was a great big loopy thing that took up half the page.

Jazz sucked her teeth. 'He gets *what*? And on a *silver dish*? You are joking! That woman has serious issues.'

'Look, it doesn't matter what we think,' I said

Hello, girls!

Just to say that I've left little Kaboodle a teensy-weensy treat as I feel so bad about going away and leaving my baby. You'll find it in the fridge on a silver plate.

It's prawns — his favourite! Give him the prawns for brekkie and then he can have a Feline Good sachet for his din-dins.

Toodle-oo!

Fenella

to Jazz. 'We are in charge of Kaboodle until Pinkella gets back, so we must do as we're told.'

Jazz rolled her eyes dramatically and said, 'All right, boss. So long as old Second-in-Command here doesn't have to touch an actual prawn. Bleurgh! I'm sure I've got a deadly allergy to those curly fishy things.'

Jazz always conveniently developed allergies when she didn't want to do something. Like the time we were supposed to be racing in an inter-schools swimming gala and Jazz suddenly developed an allergy to chlorine.

I smiled. 'You won't – I promise.'

'Leaving a bit of food out twice a day is so easy: it's cash for nothing,' Jazz said, brightening as she rubbed her hands together – and repeating almost word for word what I had said to her only minutes before. 'Yay! Just think – if we do a good job for Pinkella, she might recommend our services, and then we'll be raking the cash in! I'll finally be able to get those new trainers – you know, the ones with the wheels in the bottom and the flashing lights on the side and the multicoloured laces and—'

'I know the ones,' I cut in. I'd heard the Plan to Buy Multicoloured Trainers at least a million times before.

Jazz stopped walking. 'Sorry,' she said, looking at me guiltily from behind a curtain of hair and beads. 'I kind of haven't even asked you yet if you'll split the money with me.' She took her arm out of mine and fished in the back pocket of her jeans. 'Here.' She held out what had become a distinctly crumpled five-pound note.

I pushed her hand away and smiled. 'I keep telling you – I really don't care about the money, Jazz. You keep the down payment, and we'll sort it out when Pinkella pays us the rest.'

Jazz stuffed the fiver back into her pocket and jabbed me in the ribs, grinning. 'Hey, if you earn enough money from pet-sitting, you'll be able

to actually buy yourself whatever pet you want – your dad won't be able to stop you. It's your own money.'

I looked at Jazz and twisted my mouth to one side. 'You obviously don't know my dad as well as you think you do,' I said. 'Dad can stop me doing whatever he wants. He's Dad.'

Jazz threw her hands in the air. 'You've just got to try harder, Bertie. Try using some initiative. Sure, you've begged him and begged him for a pet and he's said no a thousand times, but you haven't thought about other ways of getting round him, have you? What about washing the car every Saturday or doing the shopping once a month or something?'

I frowned. 'You obviously don't know ME as well as you think you do either,' I said. 'I already do all those things anyway. It's called "doing chores",' I added sarcastically.

Jazz didn't have to help out around the house

as much as I did. As well as her little brother, Ty, she had a mega-cool older sister, Aleisha, who sometimes took Jazz out shopping or to the cinema. She also had an older brother, Sam, who admittedly wasn't around much these days, but he was just as cool as Aleisha. But better than all that she had a dad *and* a mum. A Full Monty of a family.

You've probably guessed by now that I don't have a mum. She died when I was really small. I can't even remember what she looks like and Dad's not one for keeping the photos out. So.

Jazz's face melted and she chewed her bottom lip. 'Sorry,' she mouthed.

'Whatever.' I shrugged. Then I blushed. None of this was Jazz's fault. I forced a smile and quickly changed the subject. 'Hey, let's go and find that gorgeous kitty. You coming or what?'

We looked all through the house and the garden, but we couldn't find Kaboodle anywhere. Jazz

gave up before I did, saying her voice and legs were aching – hilarious, coming from a girl who never stops singing and dancing, not to mention talking. I carried on calling and calling for him until I began to feel stupid.

'I guess he'll smell the prawns and come looking for them later,' I said, coming in from the garden.

I was disappointed though. The whole point of the pet-sitting thing was so I could spend some time with an actual real animal, and it was slowly dawning on me that I could go the whole two weeks coming round to feed Kaboodle without ever seeing him. Cats were like that. Elusive.

We agreed to come back at lunchtime and convinced ourselves that he would be home by then.

But he wasn't.

I began to get worried. Pinkella had made it

85

quite clear that Kaboodle liked his meals regularly, and I couldn't help thinking it was very odd that he was nowhere to be found. But I didn't want to say anything to Jazz, as she was winding herself up into a mini-frenzy and saying things like 'What'll we do if he never comes back? What'll we say to Ms P? Do you think she'll still pay us?' which wasn't helping the state of my own nerves.

We spent the afternoon at Jazz's surfing the internet, looking at missing cat websites and Googling:

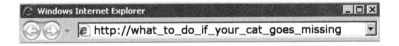

I began to feel a bit better when I saw tales of cats that had gone wandering off for a week or two and then come home just as their owners were giving up hope. But there were also reports of cats who had 'adopted' other families and started going

round to their houses for meals while their owners were away on holiday.

We decided to set off round the street, calling and looking in everyone's driveways and up all the trees in the front gardens. Luckily no one stopped to ask us what we were doing, but unluckily we did not find Kaboodle.

'This isn't a great advert for my Pet-Sitting Service,' I pointed out. 'If people hear us, they'll know we've lost him.'

'Let's go back to Ms P's,' Jazz suggested.

I nodded reluctantly. My feet were sore and my voice was sounding a bit hoarse and it was half past four already. Dad would be back soon, I thought miserably. 'By now I bet Kaboodle's sitting on one of those huge fluffy cushions in her sitting room, snoozing,' I said, sounding a million times more confident than I actually felt.

But of course, he wasn't.

'This is a nightmare!' Jazz wailed. 'And it's

definitely the hardest way to earn a fiver *I've* ever heard of. My feet are going to be so covered in blisters, forget the funky trainers, I'll be buying a pair of huge fluffy granny-slippers.'

'Yeah, right – the day I see you in huge fluffy granny-slippers the cow really will have jumped over the moon!' I hooted.

Jazz giggled but her face clouded over almost immediately and she groaned, burying her head in her hands.

'Oh Bertie, I've just thought of something! What if he's totally freaked at being left all on his owny-own?'

'What do you mean?' I asked suspiciously, thinking that Jazz was going to do her whole squeaky-Pinkella routine again.

'No, I'm serious,' Jazz persisted, letting her hands fall. She fixed me with her velvety eyes, her forehead crumpling. 'What if he saw her leave this morning and now he's decided to follow her?'

Cat-astrophe!

'Why would he do that?'

Jazz crossed her arms. 'Well, you saw those websites! They said if you move house, you have to put butter on your cat's paws to stop it running away – or was it margarine? No, it must be butter. Margarine is gross—'

'What are you on about?' I cut in irritably. 'He's not going to have gone all the way to Scotland, is he? Not unless he was quick enough to stow away in her taxi this morning, which I think is not that likely. He'll be back.'

'Oh no!' Jazz gasped. Her eyes were bulging out of their sockets. 'What if he *did* try to stow away in the taxi, and he tried to jump into the boot, and he missed and fell under the car wheels, and the taxi man didn't see him and reversed on to him and – and – and *squashed him* . . . !' Her voice trailed off in a horrified whisper.

An invisible finger traced a line up my back to my neck and I shivered.

Kitten Kaboodle

Jazz continued, the wide-eyed look still etched on to her face. 'Remember what it said in all those articles we read? Cats have a sixth sense, right? They know when something's up. Kaboodle will have definitely been freaked cos his mummsie is away. And now I think *I've* got a sixth sense about what's happened. I'm sorry to say this, Bertie, but . . .'

She paused dramatically as if she were a detective on a whodunnit who was about to announce, er, whodunnit.

'. . . considering all the evidence, and taking into account all the facts at our disposal . . . I can hardly bear to even *think* this, but I – I – I have to say . . .' She gulped and put a hand dramatically up to her throat. 'I reckon he's – oh my goodness, I reckon he . . . he's got to be *dead*, Bertie! I'm sorry, but there's no other explanation.'

Tears spurted out of the corners of her eyes and she slumped down on to one of the pink kitchen

chairs and pressed the heels of her hands into her eyes.

I stared out of the window at the cherry tree in Pinkella's garden and peered at the branches. Blimey, even the trees in her garden were pink! Was Kaboodle up there somewhere, hidden among the leaves?

'There's only one thing to do,' Jazz rasped, blinking up at me through her tears. 'We owe it to the poor little thing. After all, we are responsible for him while Ms P is away.'

'What are you on about now?'

'We're going to have to give Kaboodle a good send-off,' Jazz sniffed.

'What?' I repeated.

'A good send-off – you know, a memorial service type thing.' Jazz stood up and tore a piece of pink kitchen roll from where it was fixed on the wall. She blew her nose noisily and went on with her latest bonkers idea. 'When someone dies you have a funeral, right?' She broke off and glanced at me, blushing.

'It's OK,' I said, waving a hand at her. 'Go on.'

'And sometimes you have a memorial service – you know, you say beautiful poems and things about the person who's died. We did it for Nan. She had always loved the sea, so when she died we had a day trip to her favourite beach in Kent and we said poems and sang songs. It – it was a n-nice way to remember her,' Jazz hiccuped.

'Yes, lovely,' I said. 'But you're forgetting one small yet important fact: Kaboodle isn't dead. At least, we don't *know* he is. He's only been missing a few hours. You can't give up on him that easily.'

Jazz sniffed again and wiped her nose on her sleeve. 'It can't do any harm having a little service for him,' she said. 'And if he comes back, it's not like he'll know or be offended or anything.'

Cat-astrophe!

I shook my head. 'What is wrong with you?' I snapped, suddenly fed up with the whole conversation. Jazz jumped like a startled deer. 'The cat's gone away for a day and you immediately leap to the conclusion that he's dead? If he'd been run over we'd have seen a body —'

But Jazz was in full flow with the memorial idea, and once she's in full flow, there is no stopping her.

'Can't you just think of it as a lovely symbolic thing to do?' she wheedled. 'We could write our own poem or song, and then we'll go out into the garden and say some words in memory of Kaboodle.'

I huffed. This sounded like just another excuse for Miss Jasmeena Brown to take centre stage in an Oscar-winning performance. But more big fat tears had started rolling down her cheeks. She was getting really emotional so I thought I'd better agree quickly to her loony-brain plan so that we could get it over and done with.

Jazz perked up when I told her I liked her idea (even though it would've been pretty clear to even the doziest dormouse on the block that I really didn't) and she suggested we have the service right there and then.

'I've just had a poptastic idea!' she said, bouncing around the house with all her previous tragic misery miraculously forgotten. 'Let me just get some paper and a pen . . . right.' She started scribbling on a pink notepad she'd filched from a drawer. 'We could sing that mega song from *Cats* – you know, the musical? And we could write out an order of service.'

Hmm. She was getting really carried away now.

'Look – what about this?' She showed me what she'd sketched out:

'What does "RIP" mean?' I asked.

'"Really Important Person"; you always find it on gravestones and so on to show how important that person was to their family,' Jazz said, her eyes shining with enthusiasm.

'Shouldn't we put RIC, then?' I said.

'Eh?'

'You know, Really Important Cat?' I insisted. A voice in my head was saying, 'I cannot believe you are even having this conversation.'

Jazz shook her head. 'No, no. It's always RIP. We can pretend in this case that it stands for Really Important Pet, if that helps?'

Jazz always has an answer for everything.

'Do we have to sing "Memory" from *Cats*?' I asked, feeling very squirmy at the thought. I seemed to remember that the music went very high and screechy and I didn't think I'd be able to reach the top notes. And what if Pinkella's next-door neighbours heard and wanted to know what

we were doing? Then the cat really would be out of the bag. Metaphorically speaking, of course.

But then I noticed that Jazz had put on one of her huffy faces so I said quickly, 'Actually, I think it's going to be fab – don't listen to me.'

At last Jazz agreed that we had done enough preparation and that we could go ahead with the service. I think the fact that I kept glancing at my watch and pacing up and down had something to do with it.

'Dearly beloved . . .' she began in a droning, deep voice. She sounded like she was a grey and wrinkly ninety-year-old priest instead of my best friend. Weird bubbles of inappropriate laughter started to fizz up inside my nose.

'We are gathered here today to celebrate the life of our much-loved brother Kaboodle—'

'*Brother?*' I squeaked. 'But he's a kitten!'

Jazz shot me a dirty look and carried on: '. . . much-loved brother, Kaboodle *the kitten*. Kaboodle

91

was a kitten above all others. He will be sorely missed. In his memory, we will now sing the song printed on the order of service.'

And then, solemn as anything, she started to sing, '*Mem-ry, not a sound from the pave-ment . . .* '

I couldn't help it, the laughter just burst out. You couldn't blame me. She sounded how I imagined Kaboodle would if he'd got his tail trapped in a door, or if Pinkella had stepped on him by accident in her high-heeled spiky pink shoes.

Very soon I was howling. I just couldn't stop. I had to sit down on the bench, otherwise I would have fallen over.

Jazz was furious. 'Thanks for nothing!' she yelled at me. 'I was only trying to make you feel better. Isn't that what mates are for?' And when in response I shook my head with silent laughter, trying in vain to get my breath back, she spun on the heel of her trainers and marched out of the garden, leaving me there, gasping for breath.

Cat-astrophe!

Deep down inside I felt one hundred per cent horrendous for laughing at Jazz like that. But it was no good. I had got to that stage of laughing when you are panting hard, trying to get your breath back while vaguely hoping you are not going to be sick. I had lost control of every one of my senses. The sight of Jazz flouncing off in a huff just made it worse. I wiped the tears from my eyes and struggled to get up from the bench, and was just about to call out to her when a smooth, suave voice beside me said,

'I'm glad you find the situation so amusing.'

7

A Bad Dream?

I whizzed round so fast my head nearly flew off.

There on the garden bench beside me, washing his paws slowly and carefully, large as life and twice as kitten-like, was Kaboodle.

'Ka-ka-ka . . .' I stammered. No other noise would come out. I was sure all the blood had drained right out of me.

'Is that all you're going to say? I thought you might be pleased to see me. You two were making enough fuss a moment ago when you thought I'd disappeared for good.'

A Bad Dream?

'Ka-ka-ka . . .' I was having serious problems with my voice box. I stared at the kitten wildly. Was he really talking? I couldn't see his lips moving.

His whiskers twitched as if in amusement and his primrose-yellow eyes twinkled.

'Ye-es,' he said, talking to me as if I was a certifiable fruit-and-nutcase, instead of a very shocked and on-the-verge-of-a-nervous-breakdown eleven-year-old girl. 'I – am – Ka – boodle. Or at least, that's what Ms Pinkington chose to call me. My mother, Samirah, named me Obadiah de la Chasse. But we cats don't believe in biting the hand that feeds us, so we put up with the frankly idiotic names you humans choose for us. When you're as sophisticated as we are, you can carry off any name really. So, to put it succinctly, I won't be offended if you want to call me "Kaboodle" too. I think that poor woman thought it was a clever name – you know, a play on the expression "kit and caboodle"?' He yawned in an exaggerated fashion and examined one neat little paw, as if the whole conversation was about as exciting as a dead beetle.

I looked around, panic-stricken. This must be Jazz playing a trick on me, I thought. She was furious with me for laughing at her singing and now she'd gone and found Kaboodle and was doing that voice-throwing thing that those guys do with a puppet on their knee to make it look as if the puppet is really talking. I had no idea whether or not this was one of Jazz's many talents but at this point in my life I was beginning to believe that anything was possible.

Anything except a kitten appearing out of nowhere and *talking* to me, calm as custard.

As I continued to stare with my mouth wide open, Kaboodle stopped yawning and laughed at me. At least, I *think* it was a laugh. It was a sort of shaky, long-drawn-out miiia-oow, and he threw his head back like a human would, as if he was having a good old chuckle.

A Bad Dream?

'Your *face*!' he said, still miaow-chuckling. 'I can see you're impressed with the way I'm expressing myself . . .'

'Er, I – oh wowsers!' I gulped and stuttered and got up off the bench, edging my way nervously towards the garden gate.

This was all Dad's fault. I had spent so much time thinking and dreaming about having a pet of my own that I had succeeded in persuading myself that there was such a thing as a talking cat who could be my friend. It was official: I had flipped. Call the men in white coats, someone, please.

'Firstly,' I said slowly, trying to calm myself down, 'cats don't talk. Secondly, we – that is, Jazz – thought you were dead. So that means that thirdly . . . I must be imagining all this,' I finished up, thankful that I was alone with Kaboodle at that particular moment in time. Kaboodle looked as if I'd just waved his silver plate of prawns in his face and then run off with it and eaten the lot myself.

He opened his eyes wide and flattened his ears. 'I take *huge* offence at what you have just said,' he hissed, arching his back angrily. 'I am very much *alive and well* – no thanks to you, I might add.'

I shook my head and stammered, 'O-OK, I believe that you're alive . . . Hey! What do you mean, "no thanks to me"? What have *I* done? I've spent all day looking for you.'

Kaboodle backed up on to his hind legs, waving his forepaws at me as if preparing for a fight. 'Don't I know it,' he spat. Then he seemed to pull himself together and sat back down. 'I was trying to catnap in that tree over there after my first night of . . . er . . . freedom,' he said, vaguely waving a paw in the air. 'And then you and your little friend come crashing into the garden, screeching my name in voices fit to wake the dead (no joke intended), and then, to cap it all, that girl starts up with her hid-

A Bad Dream?

eous racket. "Memory" is my least favourite song from *Cats*. Ms Pinkington is always playing the rotten thing. Why she's so fond of it beats me. The whole performance is laughable. Humans dressed up as cats – I ask you! I mean, it's understandable that you are jealous of our sleek and alluring feline beauty, but as if *dressing up* as us could make you poor, skinny, furless creatures attractive!'

He sat up tall and flicked his tail in a way that made me think he was getting very irritable indeed. I was still in shock and did not know what to say or think. I pinched myself hard on the arm.

'Ow!' I cried. Not dreaming then.

'Tell me this,' said Kaboodle, considering me closely. 'If I'm *not* here, as you seem to think – if you *are* only imagining this – then how do you explain this conversation we are having?'

'I – I don't know,' I said, blushing and feeling very stupid. What if Jazz came back? I decided to try and take control of the situation.

'OK, so you're real. How come you can talk then?' I asked, pulling my shoulders back.

Kaboodle looked me straight in the face, cool as a salamander. '*I've* always been able to talk. It's *you* that has never bothered to listen properly,' he said carelessly.

'*Excuse me?*'

'That first time you took a close look at me,' he continued. 'Remember? Those occasions when we met on the street? And what about that time you were walking past, pushing those leaflets through the door? I stared at you, and you knew exactly what I was trying to tell you.'

I thought back to that morning only a few days ago, when my life was a lot less complicated – no Pet-Sitting Service to hide from Dad, no talking kitten to hide from my best mate – and a lot more boring, I realized, a grin spreading across my flushed features.

'Yes, I do remember,' I replied. 'You were sit-

A Bad Dream?

ting in the window of Pink . . . Ms Pinkington's front room and I felt kind of – shivery. And, er, you looked . . .' I tailed off.

'Go on,' Kaboodle prompted.

'Well, you looked a bit – lonely,' I finished.

Kaboodle nodded slowly. 'Then you *did* understand me.'

'But how can you be lonely when you've got an owner who lavishes love and attention on you and feeds you all that yummy food and loves you so much she can't bear to be parted for you while she goes away for only two weeks?'

Kaboodle wrinkled his nose. 'And how can *you* be lonely when you've got a best friend who sticks to you like glue? Not to mention a dad who works insanely hard to look after you and loves you so much that he's worried sick about you when he has to leave you on a Saturday to write an article for that newspaper he doesn't even care two hoots about?'

'How did you know about all that?' I gasped.

'You humans are so noisy,' Kaboodle said, stretching out his front paws and sticking his bottom in the air. 'It's all too easy to eavesdrop on conversations.'

I shook my head disbelievingly. 'But you would've had to be *inside* our house to hear about that.'

Kaboodle smiled again. 'No. You told Jazz all about it, and I was on the prowl in the bushes at the time. You humans are always so caught up in your own lives that you never notice what's right under your nose.'

I bristled. Up until then I had thought kittens were joyful bouncy bundles who spent their days chasing butterflies and snoozing happily on cushions. In fact, if anyone had asked me to imagine what a kitten would talk about, I would have said, 'Oh, probably just cute things about flowers and cuddles.'

How wrong could a girl be?

Kaboodle had made an idiot out of me and Jazz, skulking about in the shadows while we charged around the place, yelling his name and getting our knickers in a twist about his whereabouts. I felt my shoulders tense in annoyance.

Kaboodle laughed in that mewling way of his. 'Are someone's whiskers ruffled?' he asked. 'You even give away what you are feeling in your body language, my dear. Don't get so uptight. As it happens, I rather like you and I'm delighted that my little plan has worked out so well.'

'What little plan?' I asked sniffily.

'To get you on your own,' he purred, closing his eyes slowly and opening them again to fix them on me with a gaze that was almost hypnotic. I felt that shivery sensation trickle down my back again.

My previous moodiness immediately melted away.

I bent down to stroke him.

Kaboodle flicked out of reach. '*Never* do that without asking,' he said sharply. 'If there's one thing I can't stand it's being touched or picked up like some common little moggy.'

I started back in surprise. 'But Ms P is always cuddling you!' I protested. 'And you didn't mind when she put you in my hands the other day.'

'Yes, that was all right,' he admitted, washing a front paw absent-mindedly, 'but how would you like it if your father picked you up and swung you round the minute you walked in the door without so much as a by-your-leave?'

I bit my lip. Secretly I would have loved it. Dad had never been a big one for hugs.

Kaboodle noticed my hesitation and put his head on one side. 'All right,' he conceded. 'But what about all those times Ms P has ruffled your hair and called you "sweetie"?'

A Bad Dream?

This little cat knew me far too well.

Kaboodle waved his paw at me as if he were getting bored again and swiftly returned to the subject in hand. 'I had to get you on your own so that I had a chance of getting a word in edgeways. That friend of yours – what's her name? Jazzie-something? She does go on a bit, doesn't she? Never mind. Now that you *are* actually paying attention to what I am saying, I think it's only fitting that we should get some ground rules established. First of all, *never* touch me without asking. Secondly, I'm really not that keen on that so-called "gourmet kitten" muck that Ms Pinkington has left for me. I would prefer fresh tuna or sardines – can you manage that? Although I wouldn't say no to a bit of salmon or some more of those prawns,' he said, purring more loudly at the thought. 'Lastly, if that friend of yours sings one note in my vicinity *ever* again, I shall scratch her eyes out.'

I thought that was quite harsh. Jazz's singing

wasn't going to win that *Who's Got Talent?* show on the telly, but still! Then something occurred to me and I drew a sharp breath. 'But Kaboodle, how on earth am I going to explain to Jazz that you can, er, talk? She'll think I've gone loopy and probably send for the doctor and have me locked up.'

'Why ever would you *want* to tell her? Can't it be our little secret?' Kaboodle asked. If he had had eyebrows I'm sure he would have raised one.

'Well, I kind of . . . I sort of thought that if she heard you say something when we're together . . . well, she'd be pretty shocked,' I ended lamely.

Kaboodle gave a miaow that sounded a bit like Dad yelling 'Aaargh!' at me when he's so outraged at what I've done that he can't find the words to describe how completely exasperated he is. Like the time I put my trainers in the oven to dry out after getting caught in the rain, and then forgot that I'd put them there. (The trainers melted and turned into black glue. Luckily they were very old and

A Bad Dream?

I'd almost grown out of them. Makes you wonder what they put in trainers, is all I can say.)

'You don't think that *idiot* friend of yours will actually be able to hear me, do you? In fact, if I'd turned purple, grown wings and started singing the National Anthem she wouldn't bat an eyelid. The only thing she is interested in is getting her precious money for those disgusting shoes she wants so badly,' he hissed.

Holy Stromboli!

Kaboodle was shaking his head at me. 'Listen. Mother told me that the feline species has been trying for years to get through to humans about the way we are treated, but most people are just not on our wavelength. When it comes to cats, most humans are as deaf as a scratching-post.'

I managed a shaky laugh. 'Well, OK, I suppose that makes sense,' I said at last. Then something occurred to me. 'What about Ms P though? Can she understand you?'

Kitten Kaboodle

Kaboodle yawned and flicked his tail irritably. 'Never mind about her – I think it's time we had a little chat about *you*, Bertie.'

'Me?'

'Yes. You. I've been watching you very closely, as I said, and I happen to think I am just the friend you've been looking for, though I say so myself.' Kaboodle purred loudly and wound himself in and out of my legs, rubbing his soft fur against me.

I couldn't help smiling. This mini-cat had a mega-attitude, but I couldn't help liking him. Actually, I realized, he reminded me a bit of Jazz. I chuckled softly to myself.

Kaboodle stopped his weaving movements and looked up sharply. 'What are you laughing at?' he snapped.

'Oh, er – I'm just a bit ticklish when you do that,' I fibbed. I was pretty sure Kaboodle wouldn't be chuffed at the comparison with my mouthy mate.

Then something occurred to me. 'Kaboodle,' I ventured. 'I mean, Oba-wotsit—'

'Please – if you can't say it properly, don't say it at all,' he snapped.

I winced. 'OK. Kaboodle – erm, would you like to come and stay with me while Ms P is away?'

Kaboodle purred so loudly, he sounded like an engine. 'I would be honoured,' he said. 'But how will your father feel about that, I wonder?'

'Oh, we won't tell him,' I said vaguely, pushing aside the nagging doubts that were rushing in to crowd my mind.

'Well, you can count on me to keep my head down,' said Kaboodle, pushing against me again. 'We cats are masters of deception, you know. Now then, how about that hug? It's getting exceptionally chilly hanging around out here.'

8

Call Number Two

Kaboodle had agreed to lie low so that Dad wouldn't suspect anything. As it turned out I was very thankful that he was prepared to go along with my request, because Dad came home later that day in the foulest mood I had seen him in for a very long time.

The first bad sign was the sound of the door being slammed hard enough to wrench it off its hinges and possibly take the house walls with it. Then Dad whirled into the kitchen where I had been opening a tin of tuna for Kaboodle, scowled and banged his laptop down on the kitchen table.

Call Number Two

A panicky sick feeling rocketed up from my stomach and swirled round my chest.

'Multi-storey blinking car parks!' Dad barked. 'I've had it up to here with people who get their pathetic little knickers in a twist about things as deathly dull as multi-blinking-storey-blinking-car-blinking-parks!' he muttered crossly. 'I am a *writer!*' he carried on, as if to himself. 'I should be writing epic works of fiction or dramatic works of art to add to the nation's canon of literary talent, not scribbling ranty little columns in that rag that calls itself a newspaper!'

I let my breath out slowly and quietly and tiptoed over to put the kettle on. 'A cup of tea always works wonders,' as Jazz's mum would say.

Dad sighed loudly and shook his head. 'Sorry, love,' he said wearily, as though he'd only just noticed I was in the room. 'Bad day. How're you? Hey – aren't you supposed to be at Jazz's?' he added, squinting at me.

'Oh, I er – yeah, I *was* at Jazz's,' I began. I had my you've-caught-me-red-handed face on – a sort of a cross between a grin and a grimace.

Dad raised his eyebrows and waited.

'But we, er, we kind of had a falling out, so I came home a bit early,' I said lightly. 'I've only been on my own for about five minutes.' (Thanks to Kaboodle who'd only just gone out into the garden.)

'You girls,' said Dad, shaking his head. A smile twitched at the corners of his mouth. 'Nothing serious, I hope?'

'Nah,' I grinned, in the hope I could coax a whole smile out of him. 'You know what Jazz is like. Reckons she's our school's answer to Madonna. She was doing one of those routines again and I kind of teased her a bit about her singing, that's all.'

Dad laughed. 'You can talk, Roberta Fletcher! The last time I heard you singing in the bath I thought the pipes would burst. It was more like a

118

rusty nail being dragged across a slate roof-tile than a sweet melody of divine tunefulness.'

'Huh!' I said, pretending to be offended, but feeling myself relax at Dad's change of mood. '"Sweet melody of divine tunefulness"? Call yourself a writer?'

Dad chucked his notepad at me and I whooped and ran away from him.

'Not so fast, young lady!' he shouted, grabbing a sponge from the sink and hurling it at me.

I snatched a J-cloth and chucked it back at him and soon we were steaming round and round the kitchen table, giggling and throwing stuff at each other. It was the best fun I've had with Dad for ages.

My phone!

I froze. What if it was Jazz, calling to have a go at me? What if it was Pinkella, calling to ask about her kitty-catkins? What if it was Kaboodle – no, surely even *that* kitten didn't know how to use a phone . . .

'Aren't you going to answer it, then?' Dad was staring at me.

'Must be a wrong number,' I muttered, but just in case, I scuttled out of the kitchen and went up to my room, answering the phone on the way.

'Hello?'

'Hello. Is that Bertie Fletcher's Pet-Sitting Service?' said a man's voice.

Help! 'Er, yes,' I said, trying to keep my voice low so that Dad wouldn't be able to hear.

'Oh, good. This is Mr Smythe from number two. I received one of your leaflets a few days ago.'

'Oh, right. Bertie Fletcher speaking! How can

Call Number Two

I help you?' I tried to put my businesslike tone on, but it came out a bit shaky.

'Well, I almost threw the leaflet away, as I thought it was just another piece of that junk mail that seems to be flooding our neighbourhood these days —' Great, I'm getting a lecture, I thought glumly. Next thing, he'll be round here saying he wants to speak to Dad about how irresponsible I am and then — I realized he was still speaking, and that the tone of his voice did not seem too angry or off-putting, so I tuned back in — 'so your leaflet came in the nick of time, actually. I'm about to go away to my daughter's for a couple of days, you see, and I could do with your help. I've got two hamsters who would be very grateful if you would come and feed them and clean them out while I'm away.'

'Hamsters?' Bit of an unusual pet for a grown-up, I thought. But then I realized that this was a fabulous opportunity for expanding my Pet-Sitting

Service. After all, hamsters must be the easiest pets in the world to look after.

'Hamsters, that's right,' said Mr Smythe.

'Hurrah!' I said happily. 'I mean, er, that would be a pleasure, Mr Smythe,' I added, quickly going back to my professional voice.

'Lovely,' he said. 'Can you come round tomorrow morning? I'm leaving after lunch, you see, and I need to get Mr Nibbles and Houdini sorted out before I go.'

'Mr Nibbles and—? Oh, the hamsters. I see,' I said. And Kaboodle thought *his* name was pants!

I agreed to go round at nine, said goodbye and pressed the red button on my phone.

'Getting a lot of wrong numbers recently, aren't you?'

'Dad!'

He was leaning against the door frame, his arms crossed, and he was frowning.

Call Number Two

'Is there something you're not telling me, Bertie?' he asked.

'I, er, not really,' I said pathetically.

Dad walked over to me, tilted my chin and inspected me closely. 'Are you OK?' he asked, narrowing his eyes.

'Yes,' I lied. What with falling out with Jazz, discovering a talking kitten and trying to run an undercover Pet-Sitting Service, I was feeling just fine, obviously.

'Mmm,' he said. 'Are you sure it wasn't a bad fight you had with Jazz?'

'Noooo,' I said, putting on a 'what nonsense' expression and shaking my head vigorously.

'Is it – oh no – it's not . . . *boyfriend trouble*?' he whispered, a mixture of horror and disgust crossing his face.

'NOOOO!' I yelled. Boyfriends? Me? URGH! Had Dad even *looked* at me lately? I wondered. I was ELEVEN for heaven's sake, not a *hundred* and eleven (which is how old I will have to be before I even THINK about having a boyfriend).

Dad's forehead creased and he held up both hands as if he thought I was going to hit him. 'OK! OK! Keep your hair on!' he said, trying to laugh in a jokey way.

I glared at him.

Dad sighed and let his hands drop to his sides. 'I'm sorry, Bertie. I'm just not very good at this.' He opened his arms and beckoned to me with one hand. 'Come here,' he said.

I walked tentatively into Dad's embrace, steeling myself for a Talk.

He hugged me and talked over the top of my head at the window. 'I mean, it's obvious you're upset about something.' I cringed so majorly I thought my stomach would turn itself inside out. 'You're getting older, Bertie, and I know there are things that girls your age normally talk to their mums about. And believe me, there's not a day goes by when I don't wish with all my heart that your mum was here to talk to you. But she's not, so you're stuck with your old dad. Tell me – what's up?' he asked, pushing me gently away from him so that he could look me in the eye. 'I don't know why you're being like this, and if you don't give me any clues, how am I supposed to know how to help you?'

You could try not working so much and letting me have my own pet for starters, I thought bitterly, shrugging Dad's hands off my shoulders. But one look at Dad's face was enough for me to know I'd never be able to say how I really felt. It was my turn to sigh. Heavily.

'You can't help me,' I said finally.

'Suit yourself.' Dad tried to smile, but his mouth was too thin and his eyes weren't really in it.

Then the doorbell rang and, relieved by the distraction, I hared down the stairs to answer it.

Kitten Kaboodle

It was Jazz. And she was holding a wriggly, hissy and *very* unhappy cat.

'Kaboodle!' I cried.

'Tell her to put me down!' Kaboodle spat.

'Look!' cried Jazz. 'I found him! He's not dead!'

'No, I know – I mean, oh great – yes, definitely not dead, is he?' I babbled.

'Good to see you two are on speaking terms again,' said Dad, appearing in the hall behind me. 'I didn't know you had a kitten, Jazz.'

'There's a lot you don't know, sunshine,' Kaboodle hissed. 'For example, this vile girl is squashing the life out of me and if she doesn't let go this instant, she'll be wearing my mouse-and-vole breakfast all down her disgusting skintight jeans.'

'Oh, Kaboodle! You wouldn't!' I said.

'Eh?' said Jazz, as I gasped and clamped my hands over my mouth.

Call Number Two

Kaboodle at last succeeded in wriggling free of Jazz's tight and sweaty grasp and leaped to the ground. He then started to wind around my legs. 'Thank goodness you're here,' he purred. 'Someone sensible to talk to at last.'

'Yeah, yeah,' I whispered. 'But can you stop talking to me in front of everyone?'

'I thought you girls weren't talking,' said Dad, scratching his head.

'We *weren't*,' Jazz answered, eyeing me suspiciously.

'But we are now,' I chipped in quickly, grinning like a raving lunatic. 'We just had a bit of an argument about this cat because I said he was lost and Jazz said he was dead and—'

'Hang on a minute,' Dad interrupted, holding up one hand like a traffic policeman. 'I thought you said you'd been teasing Jazz about her singing?'

Jazz glared at me. 'You didn't *actually* tell him about that?'

127

I blushed. I was getting deeper and deeper into extremely scalding water. If I was not careful, I would reach boiling point and then probably evaporate. Actually, that didn't seem such a bad prospect at that particular moment.

Dad raised his eyes to the ceiling and said, 'You know what? I'm exhausted. I've spent all day listening to arguments and I really can't be bothered to listen to any more. Jazz, put your cat outside and then why don't you come in and sort it out in Bertie's room in front of a DVD with some popcorn or something? You can take my laptop from my study to watch a film on – you know how to work it. I'm not doing any more on it today – I'm bushed. I'm going to put my feet up and watch some telly down here.'

Jazz perked up at the mention of popcorn and DVDs, but I suddenly remembered I had to talk to her about Mr Smythe and said, 'NO!'

'What now?' said Dad wearily.

Call Number Two

'Erm – the kitten. We have to take the kitten back to where he comes from – and you don't like animals in the house, do you, Dad?'

Jazz was mouthing 'What are you on about?' at me, and Kaboodle was whining, 'Can't we go with the popcorn and DVD option? Your dad's not the only one who's tired, you know. It's been quite a day.'

I ignored Kaboodle and mouthed back at Jazz, 'Pet-sitting!'

Meanwhile Dad let out an exasperated puff of air and said, 'I don't know what you two are up to, but just let me know when you've decided what you're doing. I'll be in front of the telly.'

At least he didn't kick off about Kaboodle being there.

Jazz waited until Dad was out of earshot and then said, 'What is "peck city" when it's at home?'

'Eh? Oh – not "peck city"! Pet-sitting!' I said.

Kitten Kaboodle

A fit of giggles took me by surprise. It was quite a relief to just let the giggles take over and not have to think of what to say for a minute.

Luckily Jazz seemed to be infected by my out-of-control laughter fit and had stopped glaring and scowling at me, and soon the two of us were squeaking and holding our sides and trying to get our breath back.

'Stop! I'm going to die!' Jazz squealed.

Kaboodle sat on the doorstep, glowering at the two of us, looking very much unamused. 'When you two have quite finished,' he said sourly, 'perhaps you'd be good enough to show me to my room, Bertie?'

Dad was deep into some mindnumbing programme about DIY by then, so it was easy to smuggle Kaboodle upstairs. Jazz stayed for the DVD, but we didn't watch much of it. We spent

the whole time planning the next level of our pet-sitting empire. Kaboodle quickly bored of our excitable conversation and crept out of my bedroom window, telling me over his shoulder, 'I'm going to see some friends of mine. Don't wait up.'

Once Jazz had gone home, Kaboodle slept on my bed that night. Dad didn't find out, because Kaboodle hid until Dad had come to say goodnight, and then leaped softly and silently on to my duvet and curled up beside me on the wall side of the bed.

'What if he comes in while I'm sleeping and sees you here?' I whispered.

'Oh ye of little faith,' Kaboodle sighed. 'I keep telling you, we felines are the masters of deception. I'm mostly black – I can merge into the shadows as easily as ice melting on a hot day, my dear. And besides, humans only ever see what they expect to see.'

131

'I don't understand,' I hissed.

'Your dad isn't expecting there to be a cat in your room. He thinks I belong to Jazz, remember? So he won't see me,' Kaboodle explained impatiently. 'Now let me get some sleep, can't you? It's been an exhausting day.'

I sighed and wriggled down to get comfy. 'Just one more thing,' I said. 'Why do you want to stay here? Wouldn't you prefer to be in your own house on one of those fluffy cushions?'

Kaboodle raised his head and those spooky big eyes flashed orange in the darkness. 'Can't a cat have a bit of company once in a while without being grilled under a spotlight about his motivations?' he snapped. 'Now, goodnight.'

9

Mr Nibbles and Houdini

When I woke up, I realized that Kaboodle had disappeared from my bed at some point in the night. A twingey feeling of disappointment settled in my tummy as I rubbed my eyes and realized blurrily that he wasn't there. Oh no! What if he'd crept into Dad's room?

I scuttled out of bed at top speed and tiptoed along the landing. Dad always left his bedroom door ajar in case I had nightmares. I kept telling him I was not a baby any more, but Dad still worried about me just as if I was still a little girl. I shook my head to get rid of the confusion welling up inside me. I was not a little girl and if Dad was so worried, he should wake up and smell the bacon and not leave me alone so much.

I peered into his room.

Phew! No sign of Kaboodle. And Dad was still snoring. I crept back to my room to get dressed and realized the window was still open. Hopefully Kaboodle had simply headed out to do some prowling, or whatever it was cats did. I couldn't help feeling a bit worried for him though – after all, he wasn't fully grown yet, and I was responsible for him. What on earth would I say to Pinkella if something happened to him? She was obviously still upset about losing her old cat . . . and to be honest, I'd be pretty upset too. I'd already got used to the idea of having Kaboodle around the place.

I pushed those horrible thoughts out of my mind and glanced at my bedside clock. Eight o'clock. Jazz had said she'd come with me at nine to go and meet Mr Smythe's hamsters. I'd have no problem being allowed out – it was Sunday which meant Dad would want to have a lie-in and then read the paper, all of which I knew was code for 'I want to be alone.'

Although you'd have thought he would have had enough of newspapers for one week.

'So. Hamsters,' said Jazz. 'They're not exactly any hassle, are they? Sam and Aleisha used to have hamsters before I was born. Leesh says all they do is eat and sleep and make huge nests from bits of chewed-up paper.'

I started. 'You didn't tell Aleisha about this, did you?'

Jazz widened her eyes and batted those extra-long eyelashes. 'As *if*!'

I shook my head at her and said, 'You'd better not have, that's all. Anyway, I don't s'pose Mr S's hamsters will be that much hassle. But we'll prob-ably have to clean them out and stuff.'

Kitten Kaboodle

'At least they won't run off like Kaboodle, leaving you to fly into a frenzy,' Jazz said airily, reaching up to ring Mr Smythe's doorbell.

'Huh—!' I was about to protest that *I* hadn't been the one planning memorial services and singing freaky songs, but I bit the words back before they had a chance to escape. I didn't want to fall out with her all over again. 'Yeah,' I added flatly, changing my pout to a grin as Mr Smythe answered the door and let us in.

As we followed him into his incredibly neat and tidy house and he started chatting about his pets, I confidently repeated to myself that hamsters would be the simplest of pets to look after. They were tiny, they didn't eat much, they didn't need to be taken for walks and they lived in small cages so they were safe and sound in the same place all of the time.

However, after the list of instructions Mr Smythe gave us, I was beginning to have my doubts.

Mr Nibbles and Houdini

8 a.m. Feeding time: one small scoop of hamster mix, small pieces of carrot and cucumber in white pot.

8.05 a.m. Check water bottle is full. Do not leave too much fresh food — hamsters will hide it or stuff too much in pouches. May cause health problems.

8.10 a.m. Playtime in large cage. Clean out loo corner.

5.00 p.m. Water and food restocked.

5.10 p.m. Check for remains of food.

5.20 p.m. Feed again.

5.30 p.m. Bedtime. Tuck up tight. Avoid nightmares.

Ensure cage is shut at all times!

Nightmares? I thought. If anyone's going to be having nightmares, it's me. This guy was turning out to be more bonkers than Ms Fenella Nut-brain Pinkington.

'Why do we have to do all this at these *exact times*?' Jazz asked Mr Smythe, reading the notes over my shoulder. She stood back and put her hands on her hips, tossed her braided black hair, in what can only be described as her bored-and-totally-not-amused pose, and raised her eyebrows at me in our secret code language, which can mean any number of things, but which in this case most definitely meant, 'What kind of weirdo are we dealing with here?'

I stifled a laugh. Obviously I agreed with her, but I did not want Mr Smythe to have second thoughts about letting me look after his pets.

'It's because animals need routine, don't they, Mr Smythe?' I said, in the most sucking-up way imaginable.

Mr Nibbles and Houdini

At this, Jazz rolled her eyes so dramatically I was worried that they would disappear into the back of her head and never come back.

'That's correct, Bertie,' said Mr Smythe, twitching his nose and blinking at me through his little round glasses. He looked a bit like a hamster himself, I thought, although not as furry and definitely not as cute. 'I can see that you are just the person for the job. I am glad to know that I'm leaving Houdini and Mr Nibbles in such safe hands.'

He took his glasses off and cleaned them for about half an hour while I wondered what was supposed to happen next. Then he smoothed his small moustache carefully and thoughtfully with the tips of his long fingers. I half-expected him to reach for a carrot and start nibbling at it. What with this guy's bizarre behaviour and Jazz's freakoid zombie eye-rolling I was in danger of being completely weirded out.

Then just as I was thinking maybe I should

make my excuses and leave, Mr Smythe put his glasses back on and blinked at us as if he'd only just noticed we were there and said, 'Ah. Yes. Let's go and see the little chaps, shall we?'

He took us into a room at the back of his house and showed us the cage – or should I say the Hamster Play Park and Activity Area.

'Whoa!' shouted Jazz. 'That is some hamster home!'

'It's ginormous!' I agreed. 'This looks like some kind of Marble Run game. What are all those tunnels and things for?'

Mr Smythe chuckled and wrinkled his nose at me. 'It's rather fun, isn't it?' he giggled, blinking rapidly. 'The little chaps like to scurry around, so I bought them the tunnels and tubes and things to play in. And the wheel,' he added, pointing to a large hamster wheel about the size of a football in the middle of the cage, 'well, that's their favourite bit, I think.'

Jazz was staring, her mouth so far open she probably could have swallowed the wheel. I guessed she must have been thinking what I was thinking: all this for two tiny furry creatures the size of golf balls?

'Can you see the little chaps?' Mr Smythe asked. He pointed to a pile of shredded paper, which I had noticed was rustling gently. A tiny pink nose popped out and two shiny black eyes blinked at me. Then a brown nose appeared next to the pink nose and another pair of black eyes emerged.

'There you are, my little chaps!' cooed Mr Smythe. 'Busy bees, aren't you, with all your yummy paper? Now I should tell you how to hold them,' he went on.

In spite of all the nonsense Mr Smythe was spurting out, my tummy did a small flip and I beamed at Jazz. This was the whole reason I had thought up the pet-sitting idea. I was dying to hold one of these teeny creatures. Mr Smythe opened the top of the cage and told me to put my hand in.

'Mr Nibbles can be a bit nervy,' he warned me. 'He's the sandy one.'

I put my hand in the cage and tried to reach for one of the hamsters, but he scuttled away. I imagined Kaboodle laughing at my clumsiness.

'Try gently stroking them while they're still in the cage,' Mr Smythe was saying. 'Why don't you offer the little chaps a piece of carrot? They'll soon work out they have nothing to fear.'

I did as Mr Smythe said, while Jazz huffed and puffed and tried various unsubtle attempts to get my attention. She had obviously recovered from the shock of seeing the hamster penthouse and was now rubbing her thumb and fingers together in a very obvious we-need-to-talk-money gesture. I shook my head at her firmly and fixed my attention squarely on the hamsters.

Mr Nibbles and Houdini

'Oh!' I cried as Mr Nibbles scurried over and let me touch him while he snatched the small chunk of carrot and nibbled away at it. 'Oh! He's so cute!'

And so soft! That sounds bizarre – after all, what did I think he was going to be – spiky? But I guess I just hadn't been prepared for quite how soft he really would be. Much softer than Kaboodle, even.

Mr Smythe chuckled, showing an alarmingly large set of front teeth. 'Now gently scoop him up in both hands. Don't hold him too tightly or squeeze him! He might get frightened. That's right, you're doing fine.'

'Oh, Jazz, it's so cool! You should have a go,' I said.

Jazz sighed noisily and came over and rather limply held out her hand.

'Just remember, girls, don't get excitable when you're holding them,' Mr Smythe said. 'The little

143

chaps need you to stay calm, or they'll get nervous and they might try and run away.'

'I'm not sure I can remember all that stuff about how to get them out of the cage without frightening them,' I said, trying to distract Mr Smythe from Jazz, who was jumping about and squeaking while Mr Nibbles ran up and down her sleeves and over her hands.

'Don't worry, I've left you another note about how to handle them – it's with the food. We'll put Mr Nibbles back now and I'll show you where I keep the food and sawdust. The sawdust is for their bedding. Here is the note about how to handle them – just in case you forget,' he twittered.

He did go on a bit, I thought. Talk about Attention to Detail. I read the note:

```
Sit down while handling hamsters —
that way they won't have far to fall.
```

144

Mr Nibbles and Houdini

No squealing or squeezing. You will frighten or hurt them.

I saw Jazz was already negotiating payment with Mr Smythe. I wondered how she was going to cope with all these instructions, especially the 'no squealing' part. I read through the notes one more time and checked I knew where all the food was.

'Our basic minimum rate is two pounds per day,' she was saying.

I shot her a horrified look. But she just shrugged at me and went on, 'I hope that will be acceptable to you, Mr Smythe. It's because there are two hamsters, you see.'

Mr Smythe beamed and twitched and fiddled with his glasses and smoothed his moustache. I couldn't for the life of me think what was amusing about Jazz fleecing him for two pounds a day and talking to him as if she was the Queen and he had come to polish her boots. Mr Smythe swallowed his smile when he caught me looking, but gave me a wink and said, 'I see you have a very organized partner in crime here, Bertie.'

I grimaced. 'Yeah.'

'Well, I think two pounds a day sounds reasonable,' he said. 'I'll pay you when I get back, if that's all right. As I said on the phone, I'll only be gone for a couple of nights. In fact, if you do a good job, I'll round it up to a fiver. How's that?'

I grinned weakly as Jazz said, 'Great!'

'So, have you got any final questions?' he asked as he showed us out.

I shook my head.

'Fine. So you'll pop in and see the little chaps this afternoon, will you?' he asked.

I nodded. Then Jazz piped up in a pushy way which was becoming a bit of a habit, 'Actually, I've got a question.'

'Fire away,' said Mr Smythe.

Mr Nibbles and Houdini

'What *exactly* was the thinking behind the names "Mr Nibbles" and "Houdini"?' she asked, with a slight sneer, I was embarrassed to notice.

Mr Smythe smiled and tapped the side of his nose. 'That would be telling,' he said.

Jazz raised her eyebrows. 'Well, obviously. That's why I'm asking,' she said.

I pulled her by the elbow and said, 'Come on, Jazz. Your mum will be wondering where we are. Thank you, Mr Smythe. I'm really looking forward to looking after the hamsters. Have a lovely time at your daughter's.'

'Why did you have to be like that?' I muttered as we left.

'So*reee*,' said Jazz, not sounding it at all. 'But that man is seriously weird. What's with all that twitching and calling the hamsters his "little chaps"? He's nuts! Either that or he's a freaking hamster himself. And don't you think they've got stupid names? Mr Nibbles and Houdini. Huh! Hamsters are usually called cuddly things like Fluffy and Munchy and Hamhead,' she said.

'Ham-*what*?' I guffawed.

'Well,' Jazz muttered, scuffing her trainers along the pavement, 'if I had a hamster, I'd call it Hamhead. At least it's original.'

I couldn't really argue with that.

Jazz wouldn't stop going on about the names, though, so once we got back to her house, I agreed that we should look up Houdini on the Internet.

'Maybe he's named after someone famous,' Jazz suggested.

It turned out she was right.

Harry Houdini (24 March 1874–31 October 1926) Hungarian American escapologist and stunt performer, widely regarded as one of the greatest ever to have lived.

Escapologist? I didn't like the sound of that, somehow.

10
The Claws Are Out

After we had checked out the Internet, I remembered we still had to go and feed Kaboodle, who was probably waiting hungrily for us at Pinkella's. I'd been so caught up with the hamsters, I'd almost forgotten about him, I realized guiltily.

'I think we should go and check on Kaboodle right now,' I blurted out.

'Hey, don't get stressy!' Jazz said. 'We don't have to do everything *exactly* the way Ms P set it down – she won't know whether pussy-kitty-catkins gets fed at nine o'clock or at half past ten, will she?'

I pursed my lips. 'If we're going to do this – and

get *paid* for it —' I broke off and looked at Jazz meaningfully — 'then I reckon we should do what we've been asked, don't you?'

'OK, OK,' said Jazz. 'Let's go.'

I jumped up and grabbed my jacket. Then I hesitated. 'What'll we tell your family?' I asked. 'I'm s'posed to be hanging out with you here.'

'Say we're going out on our bikes for a bit, I don't know,' said Jazz impatiently. 'Mum's got to take Ty to football in a minute, Leesh'll be out and Sam's never around these days, you know that. And since when has Dad ever asked me what I'm up to?'

I loved that about Jazz's parents. They were so relaxed.

We ran downstairs and Jazz shouted over her shoulder that we were going out. I opened the front door and immediately tripped over Kaboodle who, it seems, had been sitting in the porch. He flicked his tail at me as I bent down to try and stroke him.

The Claws Are Out

'Hello,' I said, nervously. He really did look quite cross. 'What are you doing here?'

'I've been looking for you,' Kaboodle hissed irritably. 'I'm starving.'

'Oh, I'm so sorry, Kaboodle,' I said. 'We went round to Mr Smythe's and then we've been on the Internet—'

Jazz flapped her hands at me and shrieked with laughter. 'You kill me! Listen to you, talking to that little kitty-cat like he's your best mate!'

I gulped. 'Oh, yeah, I guess I'm supposed to do all that "pussy-wussy-catkin" rubbish, aren't I?' I mumbled. 'So, er, here, puss-puss. Here, little kitty,' I called to Kaboodle and, making a tight-mouthed kissing noise I'd heard Pinkella do, I bent down and held out my hand to stroke him. 'Shall we go and get your breakfast?'

'That's the general idea,' Kaboodle said through gritted teeth.

Jazz sighed. 'You've got no idea, have you?' she said. 'Here, watch me.' She bent down and scooped Kaboodle up into her arms.

And promptly dropped him.

'Ow! You beast!' she squawked. 'Put those claws away!'

'Tell her,' Kaboodle commanded.

'OK,' I whispered, then looking at Jazz I said, 'I, er, I don't think he likes being picked up like that. Anyway, he must be starving. Let's take him home.'

Jazz was frowning and rubbing her arm. 'He can whistle for his breakfast if that's the way he's going to behave,' she snapped.

'Just think of the money,' I reminded her. She grimaced, but followed me as I turned to go back up the road to Pinkella's.

But then I remembered something: 'I don't

have the key or my notebook. I'll have to go home and get them.'

'Don't worry,' Kaboodle purred, rubbing his head against my legs, 'I can get in without a key.'

'Yes, but how will *I* get in?' I asked him.

'You just said you were going to get the key,' Jazz pointed out, sounding confused.

I'd done it again.

'Yeah, that's what I meant,' I said, frowning.

'Trust me, you don't need a key,' said Kaboodle. 'There's a cat flap.'

'Yeah, but I can't fit through a cat fl—' I broke off.

Jazz was shaking her head at me. 'Are you feeling all right?' she asked. 'Cos once again, if it weren't a totally bonkers thing to even *imagine*, I'd say you were actually having a conversation with that kitten!'

'That's because she is,' said

153

Kaboodle, a flicker of a smile wafting across his whiskers.

'OH SHUT UP!' I shouted at him.

'Well, that's nice,' Jazz snapped at me. She crossed her arms and said, 'I've only been trying to help you. But if you're going to be like that, you can forget it. First you laugh at my singing and tell your dad about it, then you tell me off for my so-called "behaviour" at Mr Smythe's, and now you're acting freaky and telling me to shut up. Well, stuff you and your pathetic Pet-Sitting Service, Roberta Fletcher. I'm out of it.' And she spun on her funky-trainered heel, went into her house and slammed the door. In my face.

'Thanks, Kaboodle,' I sighed.

He purred, looking up at me with those golden pools of honey that served for eyes. 'Miiiaooow,' he said, making himself look cuter than ever, 'you're not going to get cross with me now, Bertie. Are you?'

My heart did a jerky leap and I bent down

154

to pick up the tiny black and white cat. 'I'm not cross with you,' I said, rubbing my face in his fur as he purred with delight. 'I just don't know how to handle talking to you while Jazz is around. She thinks I'm going loopy. Maybe I should tell her the truth—'

'No!' Kaboodle cut in swiftly. 'No, no, that wouldn't be a good idea at all,' he said. 'Now, why don't you tell me what you've been up to this morning while you go and fetch me some breakfast?'

I had the distinct impression that Kaboodle had managed to bamboozle me somehow.

Confused, I shook my head and said, 'OK – but let me go home and get the keys. I don't like the idea of trying to break in to Ms P's, whatever you say.'

Kaboodle was on his own doorstep, having a thorough wash, when I emerged from my house.

Kitten Kaboodle

'Mffffuggggle?' he said.

'Pur-leeese!' I protested. 'You could at least stop washing your – er – private parts before you start speaking!'

Kaboodle removed his head from his tail region and looked at me coolly. 'Have you never seen a cat wash before? We cats are extremely clean creatures, you know. Cleanliness is next to godliness. We always think before we act, and we *never* think before we wash—'

'All right, all right, I get the picture,' I interrupted. I was not keen to be seen hanging around outside chatting like this. I fumbled with the key and nearly tripped over the doormat in my hurry to get into the house.

Kaboodle padded softly behind me as I went through to the kitchen and quickly read through

Pinkella's notes again. He jumped and landed neatly on the work surface next to where I had put my notebook.

'So, are you going to tell me what you and your irritating friend were up to this morning?' he purred.

I decided to ignore his comment about Jazz and said, 'We went to number two – you know, Mr Smythe's?'

'Ah, yes, Rodent Man,' sneered Kaboodle. 'Half man, half mouse. Shame he's too big for me to sink my teeth into, really.'

'Ye-es,' I said. 'Although I'd say he was more like half hamster, myself.'

Kaboodle gave a funny snort, midway between a laugh and a sneeze. 'Yes, I heard you droning on about hamsters yesterday. What on earth *is* a hamster?'

I giggled. 'Don't you know?'

'No, that's why I asked,' he replied sniffily. 'I'm

157

only six months old, you know. I haven't exactly seen the world in its magnificent entirety.'

'You wouldn't know it, the way you carry on,' I said under my breath.

'What?'

'Nothing. I was just wondering how I could describe a hamster to you,' I said hurriedly. 'It's, er, sort of like a mouse, but it doesn't have a tail – well, only a very tiny stubby one. People keep them as pets and put them in cages.'

'And then eat them?' asked Kaboodle hope-fully.

'NO!' I exclaimed. 'Yuck! Who'd want to *eat* a hamster? Urgh! No, they just keep them to cuddle and play with.'

'What a waste,' said Kaboodle, obviously unim-pressed. 'So, you went to Hamster Man's house, and then what?'

'Funnily enough, we went to see his hamsters,' I said sarcastically. 'He has two: Mr Nibbles and

Houdini. He wants us to look after them for a couple of days – like I'm looking after you.'

Kaboodle paused, then did the sneezy laugh again. 'Mr Nibbles and Houdini – what pathetic names!' he said.

'Hmmm. That's what Jazz said. I'm beginning to think they're quite cute, actually.'

'Oh, really?' said Kaboodle, sounding cooler. 'So what were these un-tailed rodents like?'

'Oh, you know – furry,' I said vaguely, suddenly realizing that Kaboodle might be feeling jealous. 'And quiet. They didn't talk to me or anything.'

'Well, of course they didn't TALK to you,' sneered the kitten, narrowing his yellow eyes at me. 'What on earth do you suppose they would have to say for themselves?' He twitched his nose and bared his teeth and squeaked: '"I like carrot", "I have big teeth", "Does my bum look big without a tail?"' His features returned to normal. 'Talk to you! What utter nonsense,' he scowled.

159

I frowned. 'But surely cats aren't the only animals who can talk?'

Kaboodle preened his whiskers. 'Obviously,' he agreed. 'But cats are the only animals on this planet who have anything worth saying. Take dogs for instance – the poor foolish brutes only have three thoughts going around their brain at any one time. "Walkies! Food! Sleep!"'

I laughed. 'How do you know? A dog wouldn't want to talk to you anyway – he'd only be interested in chasing you.'

'Precisely,' said Kaboodle, blinking slowly. 'He would want "walkies", which would involve chasing me, followed by "food" – not that I'd ever give him the satisfaction – followed by "sleep" to recover from the whole riveting adventure.'

I shook my head. 'You are a funny little thing,' I said. 'Sometimes you sound like Jazz!'

Kaboodle shuddered. '*Please*! Do *not* compare me with that creature,' he said and then swiftly

changed the subject. 'Tell me more about these silent, stubby-tailed rodents.'

I wondered vaguely why Kaboodle was so curious about my other pet-sitting job, but it was quite nice to have someone show an interest in what I was up to, rather than mouthing off at me and running away in a huff.

So I told Kaboodle about our meeting with Mr Smythe and what I was going to be doing with the hamsters. 'But don't worry,' I assured him. 'It won't take up too much of my time. I'll be there for you first and foremost.'

'I should think so too,' purred Kaboodle. 'Talking of which, where's my breakfast?'

I grinned. 'OK, OK. I can take a hint.'

I went to the cupboard where the gourmet kitten food was stored and came back with a couple of sachets. 'Salmon in jelly or turkey and chicken?' I asked, reading out the labels.

'Ahem,' said Kaboodle.

I bristled. 'Listen, I know you don't like them very much. But if Ms P comes home and finds they're all still in the cupboard—'

'Throw them away,' he cut in. 'Just tip them straight into the wheelie bin outside. Go on.'

I put my hands on my hips, the sachets flapping at my sides like a pair of fins. This was ridiculous, being ordered about by a tiny kitten. 'No,' I said firmly.

'Why ever not?'

'Well, for a start it's a waste, and secondly I don't have enough money of my own to buy you all those sardines and things you asked for.'

'Hmm,' purred Kaboodle. 'I don't really care about the first reason, and as for the second – you're getting paid to look after me, aren't you? And pre-sumably for those *hamsters* as well. You must be raking it in.'

'What a cheek!' I exclaimed. 'I've already got to pay Jazz half of what we earn! I'm not spending

the rest on you when Ms P's bought you tons of food already.'

Kaboodle sniffed loudly. 'I see,' he said. 'Well, if that's how you feel, I suppose I shall have to put up with this muck.' He sat back on his haunches and flicked his tail irritably. 'Get on with it then,' he commanded.

I left Kaboodle tucking into his gourmet kitten food with more enthusiasm than I would have thought possible after the fuss he'd made. I was furious with him for being so rude. What with Jazz flouncing off in a mood again as well, I'd had enough.

11

Meals on Wheels

That afternoon I was completely down in the dumps.

Dad wasn't much use. He kept saying, 'Just let me finish this and then we'll go out and do something.' But he obviously never did finish 'this', which seemed to involve him staring at his laptop screen and muttering to himself.

So I mooched in my room for most of the day, counting the minutes until I could make up an excuse for going to feed the hamsters. I wished Kaboodle would come and visit. Even if he was rude again, it was better than being cooped up like that on my own. I hoped he might find his way

in through the window again and curl up on my bed. But he was mysteriously and disappointingly absent.

At last it was five o'clock and time to feed the hamsters.

'I'm going to Jazz's,' I announced.

'What? *Again?*' Dad exclaimed, barely tearing his eyes away from the oh-so-riveting screen. 'You two are inseparable!'

I wish.

I let myself into Mr Smythe's place and tiptoed in. It felt strange going into his home on my own like that. The house was so quiet, it was as if I could actually hear the silence. I know that sounds weird, but it was like the stillness in the grown-ups' section of the library, or in the doctor's waiting room, where everyone is sitting so still and no one feels they can talk out loud in case they disturb someone else.

I crept down the hall towards the room where

the hamsters were and jumped when my foot hit a creaky floorboard. My chest was banging and a lump had caught in my throat. I wished Jazz were there to keep me company.

As I opened the door, I heard a scuffling sound. I walked softly over to the cage and caught the tail-end (or rather, bottom-end) of Mr Nibbles burying himself in a pile of sawdust.

'Hey, little fellas,' I cooed, as I peered through the sides of the hamsters' home. 'It's only me, Bertie. I'm going to look after you while your – er – dad? – is away.'

A little pink nose peeped out from the mound of sawdust and twitched at me, then Mr Nibbles came into full view and sat up on his hind legs. He was so cute! He looked as though he were taking as good a look at me as I was at him.

I carefully picked him up and sat him in the palm of my hand and brought him close to my face.

He snuffled and wriggled a bit and then sat staring back at me.

'What are you thinking, little guy?' I whispered. 'I bet you could tell me a thing or two about Mr Smythe for starters. He's one weird cookie.'

Mr Nibbles put his head on one side and chomped his chubby little cheek pouches.

'I bet you think he's totally freakoid too, dontcha?' I crooned.

I imagined the hamster saying, 'You bet! He's a one-hundred-per-cent fruitcake with cherries on the top.'

I stroked him gently and let him scurry up and down my sleeve for a while, and then sighing, said, 'I guess I ought to put you back while I get you some food. Are you hungry?'

Mr Nibbles sat back on his haunches again and tipped his little head on one side, examining me quizzically. I laughed and went to put him back in the cage.

That's when I panicked. I had forgotten to close the cage properly while I was playing with Mr Nibbles. And now, even after I'd rummaged through all the sawdust, there was no sign of Houdini.

Suddenly his name made a whole lot of sense.

The escapologist had escapologized – well and truly escaped. Vanished. Gone. Vamoosh.

I slammed the cage shut on Mr Nibbles and then dropped to my hands and knees.

He can't have gone far, I thought, frantically scanning the floor. Maybe if I stay really, really quiet I'll hear him scrabbling around somewhere.

I closed my eyes and held my breath, all the better to concentrate . . .

Scuttle, scuttle.

There! I saw something move under the floor-length curtains that framed the French windows.

I crept as slowly and quietly as I could towards the noise and gingerly lifted the edge

of the curtain. Nothing. I must have imagined it.

Then I heard another scuffle from behind me this time. I spun round on my knees and came face to face with—

'Kaboodle!'

The kitten looked at me sheepishly and mumbled something unintelligible. That's when I noticed something in his mouth.

'Eeeek! Houdini!' I yelled. I made a grab for Kaboodle and caught him round the middle.

He whipped round and tried to nip me on the wrist, and in so doing, dropped the hamster he'd been carrying in his jaws. The poor little thing lay where he had landed, his huge shiny black eyes blinking rapidly. Thank goodness he was still alive.

I held on tightly to the kitten and hissed at him, 'I'm going to put you down – in a minute. Do exactly as I say or, boy, will you live to regret it.'

Kaboodle flattened his ears and gave the beginnings of a snarl, but quickly thought better of it and spat back, 'Don't get stressy.'

If Jazz wasn't alive and well and living just around the corner, I would have said that Kaboodle was the reincarnation of my stroppy best mate.

'Now, stay there.' I set the kitten down behind me very, very slowly, and then turned my full attention to the stunned hamster. I picked him up as gently as I could and opened the cage again, then I lowered him in next to Mr Nibbles, who had been watching the whole procedure from the hamster wheel.

I closed the cage softly and let out the breath I'd been holding.

'You,' I said to Kaboodle menacingly, 'are in so much trouble, I cannot even *begin* to tell you how much.'

The little kitten made a big show of not

listening to me, licking a front paw and slowly wiping it over one ear. Then he looked at me, all golden wide-eyed innocence, and said, 'What?'

'What do you mean, "what?"?' I growled, trying not to shout in case it upset poor Houdini any further. 'I catch you in the act of stealing a hamster with intent to murder and munch it, and all you can say is "*what?*"'

Kaboodle gave the cat equivalent of a shrug, twitching his head to one side and licking his shoulder. 'All's fair in lunch and war,' he muttered.

'You are incredible,' I said. 'These little guys are not LUNCH, they are someone's pets.'

'Pets?' scoffed Kaboodle. 'More like meals on wheels. Ha ha! Get it? Hamster wheel—'

'Very clever, I don't think.' Then something struck me. 'How did you get in here anyway?'

Kaboodle purred. 'Easy. I slipped in behind you.

171

You humans are so noisy. And so unobservant . . . as I've already told you.'

I sat down heavily in an armchair. 'Incredible,' I said, shaking my head. 'First you run off and make me – well, Jazz anyway – believe you've been run over or something, then you hassle me in front of Jazz so I end up shouting and she thinks I'm shouting at her, and now this. I'm beginning to wish I never agreed to look after you.'

Kaboodle looked down at the floor.

'And now I feel all shaky after seeing you with Houdini hanging from your jaws like that. What if he doesn't make it? You've probably traumatized him forever. What will I say to Mr Smythe? He'll be livid! And he'll probably tell everyone in the street about it and then no one will let me look after their pets, and that will be the end of my Pet-Sitting Service. Actually,' I added, 'I think this *is* the end of my pet-sitting career. It's too mega stressful.'

Meals on Wheels

The kitten padded over to me and looked up at me with a pleading expression on his face. 'I really am sorry,' he mewed. He jumped up lightly and nestled into my lap, purring like a jet engine. 'I guess . . . that is . . . I just got a bit jealous,' he confessed, nuzzling against my arm, which was firmly strapped against my chest in a defensive pose.

I sighed and shifted so that Kaboodle could settle closer to my body. 'You were jealous,' I repeated, trying to continue the tone of annoyance in my voice, but hearing it wavering as the purring on my lap got louder.

'Yes,' said the kitten. 'You see, when I saw you put that leaflet through the door, I thought, "There's a girl after my own heart – a loner, someone who will understand me." I used to live with creatures who understood me – six of them, in fact. My brothers and sisters. But Mum couldn't look after us all forever. That's the way it is with cats. Once you're weaned off your mother's milk, you have to make your own way in the world. That's how I ended up at Ms P's. And don't get me wrong, Ms P takes royally good care of me. But she goes away a lot so I knew she'd be looking for someone to leave me with. I couldn't bear the thought of being cared for by someone who I couldn't get along with. Then I saw you. And I knew right away that you would be a soulmate. That's why I behaved myself so well when Ms P introduced us. I knew she'd only let you look after me if she thought I'd be happy with you.'

'So?' I said grumpily, not willing to let him know that I was melting with every word he said. 'That doesn't explain you getting jealous of a hamster.'

'It's not just the hamster!' Kaboodle protested. 'It's you and Jazz – together all the time, telling each other everything . . .' He tailed off, looking utterly miserable.

I raised my eyebrows. 'You really *are* jealous! ' I said. 'But listen, you're going to have to put up with

174

Jazz. She's my best mate, always has been, always will be.'

'Not at the moment,' Kaboodle pointed out quietly.

'I know,' I admitted. 'But we'll sort it out. We have to. She's my best mate, like I said.' She was also my only mate. But I wasn't going to say that to Kaboodle. 'Can I have a hug?' I asked.

Kaboodle climbed into my arms and snuggled down. I would feed the hamsters in a minute, I thought, as I watched Houdini finally pick himself up and wobble over to the water bottle hanging through the bars of the cage.

At least one good thing might have come out of the rather fur-raising adventure the poor little creature had had that day – he might avoid attempting to live up to his name quite so spectacularly next time!

12

Mice Are NOT Nice

Dad was pacing up and down the kitchen when I got home. He was talking into the phone and looking worried.

'I'm going out of my mind! What if she's run away? I've been working so hard recent— Oh, thank goodness, she's just come in. Look, I'll call you back.'

He threw the phone down on to the table and ran over to me. I was horrified to see it looked as though he'd been crying. I felt a wave of sickness surge into my throat.

Oh no. I'd told him I was going to Jazz's and he'd found out I hadn't gone there after all.

176

Mice Are NOT Nice

I closed my eyes and prepared to be screamed at, but instead I felt Dad's arms around me and I was scooped up in a massive bear hug.

'Where have you been?' he mumbled into my shoulder.

'I, er, we went out for a walk,' I said.

Dad set me back down.

'In the rain? Bertie, look at me,' he said, lifting up my chin and staring directly into my eyes. 'Tell me the truth.'

This was pants. I hated lying to Dad. But then I thought, maybe I didn't have to lie any more? After all, it wasn't as if I'd been getting up to anything bad. I'd only been feeding a cat and two hamsters. OK, so one of them nearly became a hamster sandwich, but he didn't have to know that. Still, I didn't relish the thought of explaining just *why* I had decided to look after other people's pets. *Because I'm lonely and you won't let me have a pet of my own, Dad . . .*

I didn't think that would exactly cheer him up. I decided to keep it simple.

'I'm sorry,' I muttered. 'Jazz and I had a fight, and I went off in a huff.'

'What's the matter with you two these days? That's the second fight you've had in as many days,' Dad said sadly. 'Anyway, why didn't you come home and tell me all about it? You're too young to be wandering the streets alone.'

I smiled and shook my head. 'Wandering the streets!' Made me sound like some kind of smelly tramp or something.

That was when Dad snapped. 'Don't you smile at me, young lady! I've been beside myself! I've rung round everyone I could think of and I was about to call the police – you've been gone hours! You could at least have called me.'

And then I flipped too. I don't know whether it was the tangled feeling of guilt in my head, or the fact that Dad had just shouted at me, but all of

a sudden I heard myself shout back, '*Called* you? And you would have picked up the phone, would you? Cos the way I see it, you don't make any contact with the outside world unless it's to do with your horrible job! And you know what? I'm GLAD you've been worried about me. I'm glad you've actually noticed I *exist* for once! Why do you *think* I didn't come home right away? Do you think I'd want to discuss my personal problems with someone who has a closer relationship with his LAPTOP than he does with his own daughter?' I was shaking with fury.

Dad's jaw had dropped so far open I could see his fillings and the dangly thing at the back of his throat. I turned and ran up to my room and slammed the door shut as hard as I could. My head was tight and my eyes stung. I was so angry I thought I might choke.

I should have felt bad for yelling at Dad like that, especially when deep, deep down I knew he

179

was right to have a go at me. And I'd lied to him. But I couldn't hear any of those little voices in my head telling me to calm down and apologize. There was a louder voice drowning them out, telling me I had every right to be livid with everybody and everything. Including myself.

Why hadn't I told Dad about the Pet-Sitting Service when I'd first had the idea? He might have given me marks out of ten for initiative. Better than that, he might have realized the reasons behind it and started acting like a real dad for once. But it was too late now. He was furious with me. If I went downstairs and told him the truth, he'd probably only go on about how irresponsible it was to go ahead and start up the business without his permission, and then he would rant and rave about how unsafe it was to be going into other people's houses on my own. So I did the only thing a girl can do in such circumstances – I climbed the ladder up to my bed, buried my head in my pillow and finally let the tears loose, sobbing until my face ached.

I heard Dad come and knock gently on my door at one point, but I couldn't bear the thought of having to talk to him, so I pulled my pillow over my head and snuggled down into my duvet. It was getting dark outside now. I just wanted the day to end and for sleep to creep over me so that I didn't have to think about cats or hamsters or best friends. Or dads.

Eventually my tear-sore eyes started to feel heavy, and the thoughts racing around my head slowed to a numb, cotton-woolly feeling. I was almost asleep when a soft thud on the foot of my bed jerked me fully awake again. I jolted from the duvet and saw the silhouette of something pacing near my feet. I went cold and felt a scream rising in my throat when I heard:

'Purrrrr – don't get stressy, it's only me.'

'Kaboodle!' I gulped at the dryness in my

mouth. 'You frightened the life out of me.'

'The window was open.' The kitten walked up the bed and nuzzled his soft little head against my arm.

I pushed him away roughly. 'I'm cross with you,' I snapped.

Kaboodle mewed indignantly. 'Why? I gave you a perfectly good explanation about that tail-less rodent, didn't I?'

'This isn't about the hamster,' I said. 'Well, it is – but it's mostly about Dad getting cross with me, and he wouldn't have done if I'd been with Jazz, and I wasn't with Jazz because – OOH!' I shook my head. My brain was a nest of wasps.

Kaboodle sidled up to me again and purred loudly. 'Don't worry. I'll fix it,' he announced. 'Isn't that what friends are for?'

'All right,' I said reluc-

tantly, and slid back down under the duvet. Then I remembered that I hadn't bothered getting out of my jeans before leaping into bed and bawling my eyes out earlier. 'Are you staying tonight?' I asked Kaboodle, as I got changed into my Snoopy PJs.

'I'll stay for a bit. Got things to do, places to go, people to see,' he replied cryptically. 'I'll wait till you go to sleep, though.'

'That'd be nice.' I stretched and yawned and then hopped back into bed. Kaboodle nestled into the crook of my knees and curled into a tiny ball.

'Night, then,' he whispered.

'Yeah. Ni-night,' I answered.

I woke up, my heart pounding. It was Monday and I would have to face Jazz at school. I really hoped she had gone out and done something nice with her family last night so that she would have forgotten about our row. I also had to face Dad, of course.

I wished I had let him come in last night so that we could have made up.

I climbed down from my bed feeling a bit shaky and poked around in the half-light to find my purple furry slippers that are kind of like little boots and are super-snuggly. Kaboodle hadn't been able to close the window after him during the night, of course, so the room was like an igloo now. October was just around the corner, and the mornings were getting a lot nippier. I wasn't about to pad around in bare feet, that was for sure.

At last I found the slippers, under a magazine I'd forgotten about. I picked it up and leafed idly through the photos while I slid my feet into the slippers.

'AAARGH!'

There was something small and squidgy in the end!

I shrieked and kicked the offending slipper

184

across the room, and out flew something small, grey and furry with a very long tail.

'A MOUSE!' I screamed. 'A MOUSE! THERE'S A MOUSE IN MY SLIPPER!'

Dad threw my door open and ran over to me. 'What? It's all right, Bertie. Stop screaming!' he said, putting his hands firmly on my shoulders. 'That's it, deep breaths. My word, I thought someone had got into your room. Why's your window open?'

I breathed heavily in and out, and held on to Dad's arms to stop myself from falling over. I had never fainted before in my life, but then I'd never found a mouse in my slipper before either.

'There – was – a – mouse – in – my – slip-per,' I panted, pointing to the corner of the room where the small grey rodent lay, its eyes wide open, its paws held up to its face. It actually looked more frightened than me, but I wasn't yet in a fit state to start feeling sorry for it.

'Good grief!' said Dad, bending down. And

then he did something so gross — he picked it up by its tail!

I screamed again.

'It's all right,' said Dad, holding out his free hand in what he must have thought was a calming gesture. 'This little guy isn't going anywhere any more.' He didn't sound convinced, though, and he was grimacing as if he wasn't entirely sure that the mouse wasn't about to wriggle back to life in his hand.

'I'll just get rid of it, and then I'll have a look round your room and check there aren't any others,' he said, walking out of the door.

I sat down heavily on the edge of my bed and put my head in my hands. Could things get any worse? I wondered. First Mr Smythe's hamster, now this. What would that cat think of next?

'Kaboodle?' I whispered, going over to the window. 'Are you out there?'

Nothing.

Mice Are NOT Nice

'Kaboodle – was that mouse from you?' I said a bit louder. 'Because if it was I'll—'

'Who are you talking to, Bertie?'

I jumped and swivelled round like a cat on hot coals. Dad had come back into the room, and was brushing his hands together as if he was trying to get rid of something dirty. He half smiled, half frowned at me.

'Hey, I know the mouse was a shock,' he said soothingly. 'But it's gone now. Maybe a cat got in through your window—'

'No!' I cut in.

'OK,' said Dad slowly. He turned his head slightly and looked at me with a concerned expression. 'You look a bit grey around the gills, Bertie. Listen, I'm working from home today. Why don't you stay off school and have a rest?'

Wow, that sounded tempting. But I had to face Jazz sooner or later.

'No, no, it's OK. I was just shocked. It's all

right,' I said hastily. 'But – er – could you just check to see there are no more mice, like you said?'

Dad smiled and nodded. I waited until he was on his hands and knees, looking under the bed, and then I turned back to the window. I peered out into the garden, but it was still quite dark and misty. I tried looking in the treetops too, but I couldn't see anything. Certainly not a little black and white kitten.

I glanced over my shoulder at Dad. 'So. Any more?' I asked.

'No,' said Dad cautiously. 'Maybe it was just the one. Do you want to sleep in my room tonight, though – just in case?'

Sleep in Dad's room? What a nightmare! For a start, I knew he snored, and anyway, what would Kaboodle do if he came in and found I wasn't in my bed?

I laughed shakily. 'No thanks, Dad. I 'spect you're right. Anyway, if I find another one, I'll

probably scream again, and then you can come and sort it out!'

'Cheeky!' said Dad, punching me gently on the shoulder. 'Well, if you're going to school, you'd better get a move on – it's seven thirty already. I suppose I'm going to have to give you a lift.'

Only seven thirty. I had a feeling it was going to be a very long day.

13

The Cat Is Out of the Bag

It wasn't until I'd been taken to school in the comfort of Dad's car that I remembered something – in the excitement of finding the mouse that morning, I had completely run out of time to feed Kaboodle and the hamsters. Would they be OK with no breakfast? There was no way I could get to them before the end of school now.

I was so anxious about this as I walked in through the school gates, that I forgot to look out for Jazz and prepare for a sticky conversation, and instead I narrowly missed walking straight into her.

The Cat Is Out of the Bag

'Hey! Watch it,' she said, whirling round and pulling a face at me. 'Oh, it's you.'

'Yeah. S-sorry, Jazz,' I mumbled.

'About thumping into me or about shouting at me yesterday?' she asked, hands on hips. Then she flicked her head quickly and blinked at me like she was doing a double take and burst out laughing. 'Holy cow, Bertie – you look like a right muppet!' she shrieked. 'What's happened to you this morning?'

I looked up at her through my hair, which was being about as mad as it is possible for my hair to be, thanks to the mouse episode and not having enough time to even run my fingers through it that morning, let alone wash it or brush it. Talk about Bed Head. Mine was more like Return-of-the-Living-Dead Head. I looked as though I'd been brought back to life by being plugged into an electric socket.

I should have thought of something witty and

cutting to say back, but instead, I'm ashamed to say, my bottom lip actually started wobbling.

Luckily for me Jazz is my best mate, and even in one of her strops she is not totally immune to me being upset. The grin on her face melted into a creased-up concerned look, and she immediately dropped her bag and flung her arms around me.

'Hey! Hey! I'm sorry. I didn't mean to upset you. You don't look *that* bad, honest! Listen, you know I hate it when we fight.'

'I–it's not you,' I hiccupped.

Just then the bell rang, so we had to go in, which was just as well, as it had started raining, which would play ultra-frizzoid havoc with my non-hairstyle. I quickly filled Jazz in on what had happened after she'd stomped off and left me with the hamsters and then I told her about the mouse.

We filed into the classroom, me stuffing my hair into a spare scrunchy Jazz had shoved at me, with Jazz exclaiming,

The Cat Is Out of the Bag

'Guh-*ross*!'

'Jasmeena Brown — sit down and be quiet,' said our grumpy teacher, Mrs Steep. 'And Roberta Fletcher — finish your ablutions before class in future.'

Jazz and I rolled our eyes at each other and flumped into our seats. Boy, it felt good to be friends again!

The next time we got a chance to talk was at first break.

'I reckon it was definitely Kaboodle,' said Jazz, as soon as the bell went.

'What?' I asked. It always amazes me how Jazz can pick up a conversation that was left off hours or even days before.

'The mouse!' she said impatiently as she grabbed her coat from her peg. 'Kaboodle must have left it for you — it's what cats do. It'll be like a present from him to say thank you for looking after him. And no wonder — the way you talk to him, he's probably decided you're his new owner!'

I grimaced. 'I hope not.' I couldn't help thinking Pinkella would have a word or two to say about that.

'Cats are like that though,' said Jazz knowledgably. 'My aunt had one that was always bringing her dead mice and birds and stuff. Auntie Jo said it was the cat's way of showing her it liked her or something.'

I couldn't help smiling at that. It made me feel warm inside, thinking Kaboodle actually liked me. Then it occurred to me — maybe he'd been trying to say *sorry*!

'What about us?' I asked Jazz. 'Are we friends again?'

'Of course, you doughnut!' she said, nudging me with her elbow, her bangles jangling on her wrist.

'And you'll come and feed the animals with me

after school? I forgot them this morning – they'll be starving!'

'You bet,' she said. 'Sounds like you need another pair of hands with those hamsters.'

As things turned out, I needed more than one pair of hands to cope with the events that unfurled that evening . . . .

'I'll walk you back to yours,' Jazz said, as we got off the bus.

'OK,' I giggled. 'But only if you let me walk you back to yours after!'

We walked down the road, arms linked, chattering, shrieking and gossiping about our ultra-annoying science teacher – in other words, everything was back to normal. I was so relieved, my heart felt like it was inflated to ten times its normal size and might actually burst right out of me and float off into the sky like a helium balloon.

Then as Jazz and I went into my house, the balloon popped.

Dad was standing in the kitchen. He did not say hello, and he did not look happy to see me. In fact, he was glaring at me. Then he raised one hand and dangled . . . a dead mouse in my face!

'AAARGH!' I screamed.

'EEEEK!' Jazz screamed.

'And that's not all,' said Dad, as if in answer to a perfectly serious question. 'This one was by the back door, but I've also had one on my laptop keyboard, one in the kitchen sink and one in my jacket pocket!'

I had stopped screaming and was staring at the mouse in total and utter horrified silence. What was Kaboodle up to?

'It's that cat!' Jazz blurted out. 'I told you, Bertie.'

I shook my head at her quickly and mouthed, 'No!' but she didn't get the hint.

The Cat Is Out of the Bag

'I *told* you he was bringing you presents!'

'What?' Dad asked, in his slow and dangerous voice that he reserves for occasions when I am in so much trouble, I don't know how much. Occasions such as this, for example.

'Remember that cat you saw me with the other day, Mr Fletcher? And you thought it was mine? Well, I say cat, but it's more of a kitten really, and the thing is, it's not actually completely mine . . .' Jazz was babbling now, and backing away from the mouse that Dad was still waving in our faces, as if he was trying to hypnotize us with it. Meanwhile I was waving my hands violently at Jazz and mouthing, 'NOOO!'

But Jazz wasn't looking at me. She was looking at the mouse and wibbling, 'Yeah, it's definitely not my cat. Mum doesn't like them, you see. Her sister used to have one and . . . anyway—'

DRIIIING!

The doorbell. I grabbed Jazz by the hand to

stop her from saying anything more to Dad, and ran to answer the door.

'Hello, sweetie!'

Pinkella!

'What are you doing here?' I asked rudely. I couldn't help it – the words came out of their own accord.

Pinkella's mouth crumpled. 'You might well a-a-ask,' she sobbed.

Holy Stromboli! This was all I needed right now.

I would have slammed the door in her face, had she not already walked right into my house uninvited and dropping big fat mascara-coated tears all over the carpet.

Dad came through at the sound of the weeping and wailing and said, 'What on earth . . . ?'

Pinkella blinked at him through her melting make-up and waved a hand in front of her face as if to hide her distress. 'I-I'm so s-so-sorry to descend

on you like this,' she stammered. 'I'm afraid I'm having a terrible day.'

'Join the club,' Dad muttered.

I might have said the same, had I not been in full-on panic overdrive. How was I going to get out of this one?

'If it's your kitten you're worried about, Ms P, it's OK. He's probably here somewhere,' said Jazz unhelpfully.

'No, it's not that. Wait a minute – why would Kaboodle be *here*?' Pinkella asked, her voice suddenly dangerously under control and her finely plucked eyebrows meeting together in a scary frown.

By now my levels of panic had risen to completely unmanageable proportions and I could not do anything other than stare at the disaster unfolding before me, my mouth open like a frightened frog.

Dad put his hand on my shoulder. 'Bertie?'

I turned to look at him, willing myself to come up with a plausible and brilliant explanation, when I felt something soft and warm wind itself round my legs.

'Miaow? Anything the matter?' asked Kaboodle.

'You could say that,' I hissed at him, glancing nervously at the two grown-ups who were waiting for an answer from me. 'The cat is, as they say, well and truly out of the bag.'

14

Stranger Things Have Happened

'So, let me get this straight,' Dad said, sitting across from me at the kitchen table and fixing me with a you'd-better-be-telling-me-the-truth-this-time stare. 'You set up a Pet-Sitting Service without telling me, and Jazz has been in on this from the start?' He glared at Jazz as he said this.

'Yeah, I, er – actually I was the brains behind all this, Mr F,' Jazz mumbled, staring at the tabletop.

I shot her a questioning look, but she ignored

me. From the look on Dad's face, I don't think he believed her anyway. What was he going to do? Stop me and Jazz from hanging out together? Make me give up seeing Kaboodle? Put me under house arrest? Silence reigned as I struggled to think of anything to say to defend myself.

Thankfully Pinkella came to my rescue. 'I don't think you should be too hard on the girls, Mr Fletcher,' she said. 'Your daughter has actually been very resourceful, if you think about it. And her rates were really quite reasonable—'

'Her WHAT? You were CHARGING MONEY?' Dad bellowed, making all of us, Kaboodle included, jump in our seats.

'It's all right,' Pinkella said, a bit nervously. 'I *offered* to pay Roberta. It's only a pound a day, which is incredibly cheap – especially compared with the cat hotel.'

'I told you we should have asked for more,' Jazz muttered.

Stranger Things Have Happened

I held my breath, waiting for another explosion from Dad.

He shook his head at me. 'And Mr Smythe – how much is that poor man paying for his hamsters to be looked after?'

I couldn't speak. My mouth had gone as furry as Kaboodle's coat.

'Two pounds,' Jazz announced. Thanks for that, Jazz, I thought gloomily. 'There are two hamsters, you see,' she burbled, keen to make the point that everything was fair and above board.

Dad squeezed his eyes tight shut and pressed the sides of his head with his fingertips as if he were getting a headache. 'Well, Bertie, now this is all out in the open, you know what you are going to have to do, don't you?'

I nodded miserably. I did know, only too well. But Dad told me anyway. 'You are going to tell Ms Pinkington that you are very sorry for taking her money and that you will not be offering your "services" again, and you will go and see Mr Smythe when he comes back and tell him the same thing. And you will not accept a penny from either of them. Do I make myself clear? Oh, and I suppose this explains all your mysterious phone calls? Well, you can hand over your mobile right now. You obviously can't be trusted with it.'

This was excruciating. But I just nodded, fished in my jeans for my phone and made a determined effort not to catch Jazz's eye. I could just about see her from under my mad hair. She was rubbing her fingers and thumb together furiously and mouthing, 'She owes us!'

'Go on, then,' said Dad, pocketing my mobile and rocking back on his chair and folding his arms.

'I'm sorry, Ms Pinkington,' I said quietly. Then I sighed. 'The thing is, Dad, I wasn't doing it for the money.'

Dad shook his head again, this time in complete

disbelief. 'You *weren't* doing it for the money! What on earth *were* you doing it for?'

'Tell him, Bertie,' Kaboodle mewed.

But I didn't need any prompting from a kitten – from anyone, in fact. It was pretty clear to me that it was time to come clean.

'I just want a pet,' I said grumpily. 'I've always wanted a pet.'

Dad let out a long breath. 'Why?' he asked, leaning towards me. 'What's the big deal?'

I shut my eyes. 'You don't get it, do you? I need someone – something – to keep me company, Dad.'

I looked up to see that Dad had gone red and was looking very uncomfortable indeed.

Pinkella went as pink as her floaty dress and stammered, 'This – er – this obviously isn't a good time for you. You need to talk things over as a – as a family. Kaboodle and I will leave you to it, won't we, sweetums?'

'Shame. I was rather enjoying myself,' he purred, fixing me with a round yellow stare.

He might as well have scratched me – how dare he enjoy all this! I vented my irritation on Pinkella. 'Why are *you* home so early, anyway?' I demanded. 'You told me to look after Kaboodle for two weeks. It's only been two days.'

Under normal circumstances I would have been told off for speaking in that Tone of Voice, but these circumstances were so far from normal, we might as well have been standing at the North Pole in our underwear singing 'God Save the Queen'.

Pinkella fluttered her eyelashes rapidly, sniffed and said, 'There was a change of plan. That's what I was coming to tell you, before this – before your father . . . Oh, I may as well just tell you,' she said, sniffing again. 'The director who was doing the auditions for the film told me that I wasn't right

for the part.' She hesitated. 'And when I asked him why, he . . . he . . .' Her face went into crumpled-up mode. 'He said I was too – old!' she whispered, her eyes wide in horror.

Jazz caught my eye and mouthed, 'And too pink!'

The scowl on my face melted and I was overcome with a plummeting sense of guilt. Pinkella might be strange, but that didn't mean I was glad the director had upset her so much.

I grimaced to Jazz to keep quiet and said reluctantly to Pinkella, 'Oh, that's – er – that's awful. I'm really sorry. So you didn't get the part then?'

'I'll put the kettle on, Ms Pinkington—' Dad offered.

'F-Fenella,' she hiccuped.

'Sorry?' said Dad.

'Fenella – call me Fenella,' she managed, before tears welled up in her mascara-ed eyes and began trickling into rivers of black down her face.

'Right,' said Dad. He looked as if he was wishing a natural disaster of cataclysmic proportions would occur right then and there in the kitchen and forcibly remove him from this embarrassing situation.

'Bertie – we'll talk about you later,' he said to me hastily. 'Why don't you see Jazz home?'

I sighed and nodded. And then I remembered Houdini and Mr Nibbles. 'Er, can I ask you something?' I asked Dad, eyeing Ms P, who was working herself up into a volcano of tears and snot.

'Yes?' Dad snapped.

'Can I feed the hamsters before I come home? Mr S won't be back till tomorrow.'

'All right, all right,' Dad said again, pushing a box of tissues nervously at Pinkella. Her weeping had increased alarmingly in volume. 'But be quick!'

Stranger Things Have Happened

I made sure Kaboodle wasn't going to follow us. No chance of that – Pinkella had pinned him down firmly on to her lap with one bejewelled hand. He shot me a final pleading glance, but I was out of there too fast to hear him speak. Jazz and I ran out of the house, slamming the door behind us.

We raced round to Mr Smythe's, where Jazz cleaned out the cage while I kept hold of Houdini and Mr Nibbles. They scurried around in the palms of my hands and twitched their cute little whiskery noses at me.

'Poor little guys,' I crooned weakly. 'You must be starving. I'm so sorry.'

They squeaked and preened their faces and looked as sweet as ever. It was no good though, I just wasn't as excited about looking after them as I had been before. I was too preoccupied with what Dad was going to say to me later, once Pinkella

209

had gone home. And of course she would take Kaboodle with her. So that was that. No more having him all to myself. No more snuggling on my duvet in the night. The Pet-Sitting Service really was over, I realized, especially since I'd lost my phone now as well. I would not be getting any more calls and life would go back to being the same old boring, useless load of—

'Hey, don't, Bertie!' Jazz came over and gently took Houdini and Mr Nibbles from me. 'It'll be all right. Don't cry.'

I was making too much of a habit of this, I thought grimly through my tears.

She put the hamsters safely in their clean cage, topped up their food, then gave me the kind of hug that only a best mate can. 'Listen, this is all my fault. I've been a useless best friend from start to finish over this pet-sitting thing, and now I've landed you in it with your dad.'

I shook my head and wiped my eyes. 'Nah,' I

said as breezily as I could. 'This is my mess and it's up to me to clear it up.'

We finished up at Mr Smythe's and I walked Jazz home, before trudging slowly back to my place.

I went round the back of the house, as I knew Dad would be in, waiting for me. The back door was open, and as I came closer I could hear voices.

'Oh, you are a sweetie, Marvin,' Pinkella was twittering.

Pinkella was still in the kitchen with Dad! Surely she should have gone home by now?

I don't know what made me do it, but I crept quietly up to the doorway so that I could listen in.

'So when shall we get together, Marvin?'

I don't believe it! I thought. He's told her his pen name instead of his real one. I couldn't help sniggering quietly at that. Hang on a minute, though – what did she mean, 'get together'?

211

I leaned in to get my ear as close to the door as possible.

'Let's see,' I heard Dad say. 'I'm not too busy at the moment –' Not too busy? You're always busy, I thought. – 'I could do Friday after work.'

'What about Roberta?' Pinkella asked.

'Oh, that's OK. She'll probably be wanting to stay over at Jazz's anyway,' said Dad.

My stomach turned to lead. What was going on? I shut the back door silently behind me and whizzed into the kitchen just in time to see Pinkella start in surprise.

'Oh, Bertie!' said Dad, going purple as he leaped up from the table and sent his chair rocking on to its back legs. 'Blimey, you gave us a fright!'

Us?

Kaboodle was still on Pinkella's lap, curled up like an apostrophe. He yawned extravagantly and stretched out his front legs when I came in.

'What's up?' I asked.

'N-nothing,' said Dad, a bit too quickly.

'Nothing at all, sweetie,' said Pinkella, grinning wildly and cradling Kaboodle in her arms.

'Don't look at me,' said Kaboodle indignantly. 'I have no idea. I was having a lovely dream about hamsters though . . .'

'Don't—!' I warned him.

'Don't what?' asked Dad, looking puzzled.

'Oh, forget it,' I snapped and shot Kaboodle a look which I hoped said, 'You and I will have words later.'

Pinkella blushed and flicking her hair back over one chiffony shoulder, she announced, 'Well, it's been awfully kind of you to look after Kaboodle so well, Roberta darling. I've left the money I owe you on the table, dear. No – I insist,' she added, catching Dad's eye. 'And thank you, Marvin, for the tea. We'll be off now.' And she scuttled out of the back door clutching Kaboodle to her chest.

I was left staring at Dad with my hands

213

on my hips. 'So?' I demanded, once the Vision of Pink had disappeared in a cloud of fuchsia froth.

'Tone of Voice!' Dad said, scowling, which I couldn't help thinking was a convenient way of avoiding answering me.

I huffed loudly and made as if to flounce out of the room, but Dad caught me by the elbow and said, 'You have got some serious thinking to do, young lady, if you don't want to find yourself grounded for a week. You have lied to me and put me in a very difficult and embarrassing position. You are lucky Fenella is such a kind and gener-ous person —' What do you know about *Fenella*? I thought. — 'and now you should go to your room. Surely you've got some homework to do or some reading or something?'

Dad needn't have worried. I was already on my way up the stairs. It was pretty clear he had not listened to a word I'd said in the past twenty-four

hours. He didn't care whether I wanted a pet or not, he didn't care I had no one to talk to at home, he didn't care that I was fed up with him never being around, and now he was agreeing to spend his spare time with Pinkella the Poodle instead of with me – HIS ONE AND ONLY DAUGHTER!

Why had they agreed to meet on Friday – without me around?

And more importantly, why did she and Dad jump apart as though they'd been electrocuted when I walked into the room? They'd only just met, for goodness sake.

Surely my dad wasn't . . . No.

I shook my head rapidly to try and make the idea go away. But it wouldn't. It had well and truly lodged itself in my mind.

Was Dad going on a DATE with the Vision of Pinkness?

A searingly bright image filled my head of Pinkella and my dad walking into the sunset

215

together with romantic music in the background and little bluebirds twittering around their heads as they gazed deeply into each other's eyes.

I wished the house would fall down on top of me and squash me flat.

15
A Purr-fect Spy

The only way I could find out what Dad and Pinkella had planned for Friday night was to enlist the help of someone who could listen in without being noticed. And I figured that after the hamster incident, not to mention the many dead rodent incidents, Kitten Kaboodle owed me one.

So I went to the window and called for him, hoping that he might hear me from across the road and come running. (And very much hoping that he would still want to talk to me now that Pinkella was back.) And then I climbed up on to my bed, lay on my front with my feet at the pillow end and waited. I watched the last wisps of the October

217

evening light leak out of the sky and stared at the trees as they turned into shadows of their former selves. My mind wandered over the events of the past few days and I let my mind drift as I waited.

Thud.

A soft dark shape appeared on the ledge outside my window.

I grinned and clambered down my ladder to let him in.

'It was a little difficult to get away,' Kaboodle murmured, rubbing his head against my arm. 'Ms P was still quite upset about that dreadful director being so rude to her, so she needed a few more hugs than usual, and a friendly shoulder to cry on, so to speak. However, I heard you call – so, what's the matter?'

'We're going to have to stop them.'

'Stop who? From doing what? You're going to have to be more precise,' Kaboodle said.

A Purr-fect Spy

I tutted. 'Dad and Pinkella — they've got a date on Friday night, haven't they?'

'They have?' Kaboodle asked.

'You know they have! You were in the room when they were arranging it!'

'I told you, I was sleeping—'

'No. I don't buy that. I know "you cats" only ever sleep with one eye shut,' I said, my voice edged with sarcasm.

'Ah,' Kaboodle said. He washed a paw infuriatingly slowly and then said, at last, 'Still, I don't see how I can be of any help.'

'Well, I do! You are in the perfect position to spy on them on Friday night. I want you to watch everything that they say and do and come and tell me about it. I don't care if you have to come and tell me at Jazz's. I don't care if she thinks I've gone mad having a conversation with a cat. I need to know what's going on and I need to be able to stop it. I cannot have Pinkella Deville going out with my dad!'

'Why ever not?' Kaboodle asked, puzzled. 'She's a lovely woman. Could do with a few tips on improving my diet, I'll grant you, but other than that she's kind, cuddly, concerned—'

'And a complete nut-head!'

Kaboodle tilted his little head to one side and flicked his ears forward. I could have sworn he was frowning at me. 'Bertie Fletcher, I do not understand you.'

Join the queue, I thought.

'You say your dad's lonely and all he ever does is work—'

'I never told you that!' I cut in.

Kaboodle raised a paw as if to stop me. 'You didn't have to,' he said. 'It's obvious.'

'Don't tell me – body language,' I huffed.

'That and my extraordinary powers of feline perception,' Kaboodle agreed. 'So, as I say, it's pretty obvious you're worried about your father, and now that he is showing interest in a perfectly lovely lady—'

'Listen,' I said sharply, not wanting to hear another word. 'Pinkella may be *lovely*, but she is just not the sort of person I want hanging around my dad, OK? She's fussy, and la-di-dah, and – oh, can't you see it would be mortifying to have her turn into a permanent fixture in my life, floating around the place in all that fluffy pink rubbish and going on about everything being "gorrrrgeous" and calling me Roberta . . . ?' I tailed off angrily.

Kaboodle eyed me carefully. 'All right,' he said. 'I'll report back on your father's meeting with Ms P. But just do me one little favour – try not to get things out of proportion. There's bound to be a simple explanation for all this.'

Friday took its time coming. Friday usually does, of course, because it is the best day of the week

– no homework to do in the evening, great telly, no alarm clock the next morning, and the whole weekend to look forward to. But this Friday was different. I was seriously concerned about my dad spending any time at all with that Profusion of Pinkness, let alone on a Friday night, which any idiot could tell you was a night for dating and going out with girlfriends and boyfriends.

There had been a lot of worrying developments that week. Dad had been acting like a total weirdo – or, should I say, even more of a weirdo than usual. He had become ultra-dreamy, that's the only way to describe it. He hadn't even hassled me once about my homework, or checked my spellings or anything. Normally I would not complain about this, of course, but he was being just so ... un-Dad-like. He would sit down to eat supper with me, for example, and he'd take up his fork to start twirling his spaghetti, and then it was as if he'd completely forgotten where he was or what he was supposed

222

to be doing. He would sit there, the forkful of pasta hovering in front of his mouth, and he'd stare off into the distance. It would take quite a lot of me saying 'Dad – Da-a-ad! Is there anyone there?' and flapping my arms around in front of his face to get his attention.

I was convinced all this dippy behaviour was because Dad's mind was on other things. Other *pink* things.

After school that day, I finally plucked up the courage to tell Jazz about my horrifying suspicions.

'Jazz . . . I think . . . I cannot believe I am saying this . . . I'm really worried Dad might have fallen in *love*!' I spoke in hushed tones. 'With . . . Ms P!'

'Oh good grief alive, I hope not! She is one spooky lady!' Jazz shrieked. 'I reckon she is either completely off her rocker or she is an undercover agent for a secret organization and is posing as someone who is completely off her rocker. For a start, no one who is sane wears that much pink unless they're two years old and still believe in fairies. And for a finish, that perfume is so strong I suspect it might actually be some kind of poisonous fumigation weapon that deals a slow but deathly blow to whoever comes near it.'

I curled my lip and tutted. Jazz loves a good conspiracy theory. She was always going on about undercover agents and secret organizations and deathly weapons. She was convinced that half of the teachers at our school were spies. I kept telling her that they were all too boring and badly dressed to be super-slick double agents, but she wasn't having any of it. She said that was the whole point and she said it again now.

'You always think that spies are like the people in films and on the telly – that they're all good-looking and dress in really posh clothes and raise their eyebrows a lot,' she went on accusingly. 'But they are absolutely *not* like that. If they were, then

everyone would know that they were spies and there'd be no point in them trying to go under-cover. No, real spies are exactly like Pinkella – the most useless person in the world that you can think of on the surface, but underneath, they can speak thirty-two languages and are pretty mean with their fists.'

My mind boggled a bit at the idea of Pinkella being pretty mean with her fists.

'It's like Mr Smythe,' she went on, warming to her theme. 'He has to be a spy. All that acting-like-his-hamsters thing that he does is just a front. He's probably super-brainy at maths and goes round the world cracking codes and solving mysteries. He looks enough of a geek. And those hamsters are probably trained to carry ultra-teeny computer chips around in their pouches for him. I bet that's why Houdini is such a brilliant escapologist. And another thing, I don't even believe that Mr S was at his daughter's. Did you notice he changed his story when we went round to say "sorry" for taking his money —' her voice had turned very sour at the memory — 'and said he'd been to an *art exhibition*?'

'That's not changing his story!' I cried. 'He could easily have gone to an art exhibition *with* his daughter. Anyway,' I said, feeling quite exasperated, 'you are not taking my problems seriously. There's a lot more worrying me than the idea of Ms P as a weird pink super-spy or Mr S as a brainy geekoid-hamster-head. What if my dad *has* fallen for Pinkella?'

Jazz shuddered. 'We will have to do some investigation,' she said. 'I'm sure you are wrong. I know your dad is a bit bonkers, but even he could not possibly fancy someone who thinks chiffon is acceptable daywear . . .'

I stopped Jazz before she could develop her conspiracy theory any further. 'Listen, I'll see you in a bit,' I said. 'I'm just going to whizz home to grab a few things for our sleepover and get changed.'

226

A Purr-fect Spy

I needed space to think before that night.

I hadn't seen Kaboodle to talk to that week. It had made me pretty sad and actually a bit annoyed too. He could have come round if he'd wanted to, even if it was just to curl up on my bed at night. But now that Pinkella was back, he was spending all his time at hers, probably being hand-fed prawns and tuna and snoozing all day on a velvet cushion while Pinkella stroked him and told him how she couldn't live without him. An unpleasant image exploded into my brain of my dad being hand-fed by Pinkella while he lazed around on a velvet cushion. A wave of disgust rolled over me, and with it came a sudden, worrying thought: what if Pinkella could understand Kaboodle as well as I could? What if Kaboodle had told her all about me and was right now sharing all my deepest darkest secrets? What if they were both laughing at me, while Pinkella hatched a wicked plan to steal my dad away from me with Kaboodle's help?

227

Kitten Kaboodle

No doubt about it, I was going crazy. I had to talk to Kaboodle before he went undercover that evening as Super Spy Cat.

I rang Pinkella's doorbell.

'Oh, hello sweetie! What are you doing here? Is there a problem about tonight?'

I grimaced and then quickly tried to grin instead. 'No, no. I was just, er, wondering if I could see Kaboodle?'

Pinkella clasped her hands together in front of her and cooed, 'Oooooh, that is sooooo adorable! Do you miss him, darling?'

I nodded, not trusting myself to speak in case I said something rude.

'Of course you can see him! The little puss-cat is snoozing in the sitting room on his favourite chair. In you go. I'll leave you to it, if you don't mind. I was just about to get ready.'

I nodded again and muttered, 'Thank you.' Get

ready? I wondered how long it would take her to choose her outfit. 'Now let me see, shall I wear the pink or the, er, pink?' It would be funny if it wasn't actually so tragic.

I went into the sitting room and sure enough, Kaboodle was asleep, folded in on himself in a neat little parcel, his tail wrapped securely around his tiny fluffy body, his eyes shut tight. At first glance he could have been a black velvet scarf or a black jumper, thrown on the chair in a heap. It was only when he opened one amber eye that I could make out where his body ended and his head began.

'Hello!' he drawled, raising his head very slightly and blinking slowly. 'Long time no see.'

'Yeah, well, that's not my fault,' I said, sounding crosser than I'd planned.

Kaboodle stared back at me in silence. I shifted uncomfortably, regretting my outburst. I tried again. 'What I mean is, I've kind of missed you, I guess.'

Kaboodle let out one of his jet-propelled purrs,

and I'm sure he smiled too. 'Well, that's funny, because, in a strange way, I suppose I've missed you too.'

'Why haven't you been to see me then?' I demanded, the stress rising in my voice and catching.

Kaboodle stood up and arched his back in an exaggerated stretch as though he had been asleep for years. 'Aaah, that's better,' he said. 'Hmm, what did you say?' He must have caught a look in my eye that stopped him from procrastinating further and quickly sat down, saying, 'Yes, I'm sorry I haven't been round since Ms P came home. You see, it's rather difficult; she keeps quite a tight rein on me. If I slipped over to your place for any length of time, she would worry terribly.'

'Poor Ms P,' I said, a flash of steel in my voice.

A Purr-fect Spy

'Yes,' said Kaboodle mildly. 'So, what was it you wanted to see me about?'

'Well, excuse *me*, I didn't realize I needed a reason!' I huffed. 'But if you must know, I wanted to talk to you about – her and, well, you know,' I faltered. I couldn't even bring myself to say the words out loud.

Kaboodle jumped down from the chair and came over. 'Oh, that. Well, don't get *stressy*,' he purred, pressing himself against my legs.

I sat on the chair he had been sleeping on. The cushion was warm where Kaboodle's body had left a small indent. I sank back against the pink velvet and he jumped up on to my lap.

I asked him if he had any further information for me.

'Have you overheard any suspicious phone calls this week?' I pressed him.

At first I thought he wasn't at all interested. He purred as I stroked his soft black coat, his eyes

half-closed. I hoped he wouldn't go back to sleep
again.

Eventually he sat up and gave his chest a quick,
efficient lick. Then he said, 'Actually, I have noticed
quite a few strange goings-on since I was last at
your place. I'm afraid you're probably right to be
worried, Bertie. Your dad is definitely not himself
these days.'

I started. 'What sort of goings-on?' I asked. 'You
haven't even been to our place this week.'

Kaboodle yawned. 'You humans miss out on
so much important information,' he said. 'So busy,
rushing here, rushing there. I hadn't forgotten your
request to spy on your father, you know. All it takes
is a little subtlety, a little cunning and common
sense—'

'OK, OK! So you keep saying. Less of the
lecture, thanks,' I muttered. 'WHAT important
information have you gathered?'

Kaboodle made a small coughing noise as if he

was clearing his throat. 'Well, for a start he keeps disappearing off into his study and pacing the floor and muttering to himself.'

I laughed, feeling a bit relieved. 'That's nothing new! Dad's a writer – it's what writers do!'

Kaboodle looked rather offended. 'And what about that disgusting food he's been cooking? How do you explain that?'

That was certainly true – and out of character. Dad was usually a fantastic cook, but that week . . .

'He put sugar in the bolognaise sauce last night, I noticed,' Kaboodle persisted.

Dad had been halfway through cooking the sauce and he'd reached into the cupboard to get out some seasoning – salt, pepper, herbs and spices and that – and he'd just grabbed the first thing he'd laid his hands on, which in this case had been sugar, and he'd chucked it in without looking.

'Yeah,' I agreed glumly. 'And you know what was even weirder? He ate it all without even noticing how gross it tasted.'

There had been some other totally weird concoctions that came about in a pretty similar way, such as tomato sauce with sugar and sliced mango, apple crumble with baked beans, and peach and rice soup. I had offered to take over the cooking, but Dad had simply looked bewildered and asked, 'Why?'

'Listen to me,' I said decisively. 'We've got a situation on our hands. Dad is either going loopy-loony on me, or he's falling in love, which in any case amounts to the same thing as far as I'm concerned, and I want you to help me do something about it!'

Kaboodle stopped purring and looked at me as if he was actually paying attention for the first time.

'The way I see things,' I continued, taking

advantage of the fact that I had his full attention for once, 'you owe me a few favours. I looked after you and fed you and let you sleep on my bed while Pinkella was away, and you've done nothing in return except get in between me and Jazz and then deposit dead mice all over the house—'

'You call that *nothing*?' Kaboodle butted in. 'There are cats not half as good-natured as I who would not even *entertain* the idea of bringing you such delicious morsels as—'

'All right, all right,' I said impatiently. 'Just listen, for goodness sake! I'm really worried about Dad and there is no way I'm ever going to know exactly what goes on tonight as I've got to go to Jazz's for a sleepover. So I'm relying on you. Please, Kaboodle. You said you would go over there and watch them.'

The kitten licked his lips and then set to work on his front paws. I started tapping my foot impatiently. This 'washing before you think'

business was all very well, but it was getting on my nerves . . .

'All right,' said Kaboodle suddenly.

'Thank you,' I said, relief flooding my voice. 'And will you come and report back to me exactly what was said?'

Kaboodle flattened his ears. 'I'm not coming to Jazz's house!' he protested. 'That girl will pick me up and fling me around and then that odious brother of hers – what's his name? Little Tike?'

'Tyson.'

'Yes. *Tyson* will probably decide to use me as a slingshot or something equally insane. Anyway, we can't talk in front of anyone, remember?' he added – a bit sarcastically, I thought.

'Can't you come in through a window once we're asleep?' I asked. 'You could wake me up quietly like you've done before. Jazz sleeps so deeply,

she won't hear you. She could sleep through a hurricane, that girl.'

Kaboodle agreed reluctantly. I got off the sofa with him in my arms and placed him carefully back on the cushion. He looked up at me, and with a final purr and a rub of his head against my hand, he miaowed, 'See you later,' and settled back to sleep.

Thank goodness for Kaboodle, I thought as I called out a goodbye to Pinkella and dashed home to get changed. With him on my side, I'd soon have Dad back for myself and away from that woman. Everything was going to be all right. Wasn't it?

16
Midnight Prowler

Jazz and I always had a laugh at our sleepovers – especially when they were round at hers. Her mum was so cool – she let us watch loads of DVDs and have midnight feasts. Sometimes if Aleisha was in she'd paint our nails for us and do our hair in funky styles. She's the only person who's ever been able to make my hair look cool.

This time, however, I was not too keen on doing any of that stuff or staying up late, as I was worried that it would mean Jazz would still be awake when Kaboodle arrived. So when we'd finished watching Jazz's favourite DVD, *Summer School Dance Camp*, sung all the songs, done all the dance routines and eaten our way through four packets of popcorn, two packets of marshmallows and one tube of prawn cocktail Zingles crisps, I stretched and yawned in an overenthusiastic kind of way and said, 'Oh boy, you know, I'm soooooo tired. Shall we go to bed now?'

'*What?*' cried Jazz. 'But we haven't watched the extra scenes yet or seen the interview with Zeb Acorn.'

Zeb is the lead actor in *Summer School Dance Camp* and Jazz's all-time hugest *lurve*-crush and she's going to marry him, once she's figured out how to actually get to meet him.

'I know, but we've watched this film fifty zillion times before, and I'm really, really tired,' I yawned again. 'I've had a big week.'

Jazz pursed her lips. 'So sorry you're finding everything so *bor*-ing,' she huffed. 'I thought you'd want to do stuff to take your mind off your dad and Ms P and . . .' She caught sight of me

239

staring at her in disbelief. 'Sorry. I didn't mean to talk about that. You're probably right. I'm tired too. It is eleven already.'

I smiled. 'Thanks, Jazz.' Part of me felt a bit guilty that Jazz was trying to be nice, when the real reason for getting to bed earlier than usual was that I wanted her out of the way.

We called out goodnight to Jazz's mum and dad who were downstairs watching telly, and then got comfy on the bunk beds. As a treat, Jazz let me sleep on the top. 'You need cheering up,' she said.

The top bunk was definitely the best, probably because it felt like my bed at home. Also there were these wicked fairy lights that Jazz had wound around the top of the bunk and down the sides, so even when all the house lights were off, her room was still lit up with a warm glow. It was comforting and cosy. Sometimes we snuggled up together on the top bunk until we started drifting off and talking nonsense and then I would climb out and go to

sleep on the bottom bunk. But tonight, we got into our own beds and Jazz talked up to me through the bluish-purply glow.

'Bertie?' she said tentatively.

'Hmm?'

'Don't shout at me, but I've been wondering, would it really be so bad if your dad and Ms P get together?' she asked.

'Wha—?!'

'Just listen a minute,' Jazz interrupted. 'I know she's a bit bonkers and everything, but she's not actually mean or evil, is she? And if she makes your dad smile, that can only be a good thing, can't it?'

'No. It won't work,' I said simply. Jazz stayed quiet, but her silence was full of doubt. 'It won't!' I repeated more loudly. 'I won't let it. What if they got really serious about each other? If Dad's going to find a new partner, I ought to have a say in it – whoever he ends up with will be my MUM,

Jazz! He can't just go and fall in love with whoever he likes. Are you really saying you wouldn't care who your dad ended up with if *your* mum died?'

'I'm not sure it works like that,' she said. 'Anyway, I think you're getting it a bit out of proportion. This is only their first date — if that's what it is,' she added hastily.

I thumped back on to my pillow with my hands behind my head and went into major-sulk-mode. Why wasn't Jazz taking this seriously? How could my best mate not be on my side? I angrily waited for her to apologize. To say something — anything — to make me feel better.

But all I heard was a light snoring.

I, on the other hand, couldn't sleep at all. My heart was banging in my throat, and my head was fizzing with worries about what Kaboodle would have to report when he finally turned up. I was

trying to dream up a scenario where I could find out something terrible about Pinkella's past and engineer a way for Dad to stumble across it, and then Pinkella would be so embarrassed she'd have to move away. But then I wouldn't see Kaboodle again . . . My brain was whirring round and round, with no solution in sight, and I was about to get up and go and fetch a glass of water when there was a scratching at the window and a yowling, mewling noise.

Kaboodle!

I scrambled down from the top bunk and managed to bang my knee on the way. The ladder knocked against the side of the bed and made a noise like a hammer against rock in the silence of the sleeping house.

'Don't make me eat the peas!' said Jazz, sitting up in bed and staring at me with scarily zombie-like open eyes.

Freaky! She had never talked in her sleep

243

before! I stuffed my hand into my mouth to stop myself from laughing, and then whispered, 'It's OK, Jazz. Go back to sleep.'

Thankfully she did, so I crept over to the window and let a very bedraggled and unhappy kitten into the room. His fur was spiky and matted against his tiny skinny body and his whiskers were drooping. He shook each paw delicately and disgustedly as he crossed the windowsill and I realized that he was dripping wet.

'Kaboodle! Are you all right? What's happened to you?' I tried to pick him up and comfort him, but of course he didn't want that. He gave himself a shake and then set about washing his ears slowly, as if to cover up his embarrassment at arriving in such a state.

'Aren't you going to tell me what happened?' I persisted, fetching my flannel from my overnight bag. I made as if to wipe him down, but he gently backed away from me, opened his mouth and gave

a huge yawn, showing off all his needle-sharp teeth and his small pink tongue.

'I had a bit of an accident while doing your dirty work,' he said, sounding as if the whole thing left him bored to tears. He set about grooming his back so that he didn't have to catch my eye.

'Oh, come on, Kaboodle!' I cried. 'What happened?'

Kaboodle sat up straight and fixed me with his round yellow eyes. 'Promise you won't laugh,' he said.

'Promise,' I said. With his permission I picked him up and we climbed to the top bunk and snuggled down together. It wasn't the greatest of kitty snuggles, what with his fur being wet and everything, but my heart still fluttered happily having that little cat all to myself again.

Kaboodle's voice settled into a low purr as he quietly explained what had happened.

'I thought I would get a good view into the

room from the tree outside your bedroom window,' he explained. 'Unfortunately . . .' He stopped purring and gave an embarrassed sort of cough. 'I – er – aimed rather too high.'

'What do you mean?' I asked.

Kaboodle flattened his ears impatiently. 'I couldn't see properly when I was at the same level as the kitchen, which is where they were, so I thought I would climb further up and look down on them instead. The trouble is, the best branches were a little higher than I thought . . .'

I smirked. 'You got stuck,' I said.

'Excuse *me*,' said Kaboodle irritably. 'You promised you wouldn't laugh.'

I bit the insides of my cheeks and nodded.

'So, I got stuck,' Kaboodle went on in a tight-lipped way, 'and I, well, I suppose I panicked. In fact, I cried out for help, if you must know,' he added.

'And?' I prompted, digging my fingernails into the palms of my hands.

246

Midnight Prowler

'Ms P heard me, of course,' he said, gritting his teeth. 'She would recognize my voice from a mile away. She came out, flapping and wailing and protesting that I would never be able to get down. Nonsense, naturally. We felines always get out of scrapes of our own accord in the end – it just takes a little time. Anyway, Ms P got your father to come out and try to save me – all well and good, except, of course, your father is about as much use as a kipper in a kettle when it comes to saving anyone. He doesn't like heights, does he? So he wasn't about to climb up a ladder and try and get me the conventional way. Oh no. Especially as apparently it was "too dark" for that. He decided it would be a good idea to go to the upstairs window, lean out and tie a length of rope to the branch I was hanging from, because apparently it would be simple for me to walk to the edge of the branch and in through the open window.'

'Sounds brilliant,' I said.

'Yes, he's quite the genius, isn't he, your dad?' asked Kaboodle, his voice drenched in sarcasm. 'And I'm sure his amazing brainwave would have worked too, except that Ms P distracted him, didn't she? She was frightened your father was about to fall out of the upstairs window, so she made a lunge for his legs and yelled to him not to lean out too far. He promptly lost his footing and let go of the rope; the branch pinged back, and I went flying over the wall, crashed into the washing that your next-door neighbour had stupidly left out overnight and ended up in the fish pond with a pair of outsized lacy knickers wrapped around my head,' Kaboodle ended grumpily.

As Kaboodle's description reached its conclusion, I bit down on my lip and tried hard to focus on breathing, so that the tidal wave of laughter forcing its way up inside me would not explode and wake Jazz. But as soon as Kaboodle mentioned the word 'knickers', I lost control and couldn't hold

it in any longer. I collapsed into hysterics, clutching my sides and hooting until I couldn't breathe.

'Oh! Oh! That is just too hilarious!' I eventually managed to squawk.

There was a thump from under me as I realized too late that Jazz was stirring.

Kaboodle shot me a look of pure disgust and leaped back on to the windowsill.

'Hey, come back!' I hissed. 'What about Dad? Did you see what he and Ms P were up to?'

Kaboodle was already halfway out of the top window, his front paws gripping on to the opening, his back legs dangling and scrabbling to get himself free. He glanced back at me and spat, 'As if I'm going to tell you now! I don't appreciate being laughed at, you know.'

'Hey, what's up?' came a blurry voice from below.

'It's nothing,' I said quietly. 'I just had a night-mare. I'm OK now. Go back to sleep.'

'*You* had a nightmare?' Kaboodle sneered, as he finally managed to get a grip and flipped himself out of the top of the window. 'The nightmare's only just begun, my dear,' he mewed as he disappeared from sight.

What did that mean?

'Don't go!' I called.

Too late. He'd gone.

Suddenly Jazz was out of bed and peering at the window in the gloom. 'I heard a noise. Did you hear a noise? What if it's a burglar?'

'A cat burglar more like,' I muttered.

'What?'

'Nothing. Really, it's nothing, Jazz. I told you – I had a nightmare. I couldn't sleep so I went over to the window to look at the moon and stuff.'

Jazz was still only half awake, luckily for me, so she padded back to her bed and mumbled some-

thing about it being freezing. Within seconds snoring wafted up again from the bunk below. I crept down the ladder again and tiptoed over to the window. 'Kaboodle?' I whispered.

Nothing.

I tried again, but I didn't want to risk waking Jazz, so I couldn't raise my voice enough to make myself heard.

I sadly turned from the window and started back to bed, when I heard a tiny mew from behind one curtain and Kaboodle stuck his head out.

'Thank goodness!' I whispered, turning round. 'I thought you'd left.'

'Oh, sorry? Did you want to *talk* to me? I thought I was only good for a bit of fun – an hilarious event to be LAUGHED at,' Kaboodle spat.

I bit back a hasty retort. I didn't want to start another argument.

'Sorry,' I mumbled. 'I didn't mean to offend you.' Then, because I really needed to get back to the matter in hand, 'So, where were we?'

Kaboodle purred to acknowledge my apology.

I let him walk into my arms and carried him gently back to bed. We snuggled into the comfy position we'd been in before and Kaboodle quietly said, 'I'm afraid you are not going to like this, Bertie, so please don't get cross with me like you did last time.'

I gulped. My throat was dry. I wished I had got that glass of water after all. 'OK,' I muttered.

Kaboodle's tail twitched and he looked up at me, fixing me with those deep pools of honey. 'I'm sorry, Bertie, but I think you were definitely right to be worried.'

My eyes prickled and I swallowed hard.

Kaboodle went on hastily. 'And I think it's serious – I heard them talking about spending more time together and how important it was to "see this thing through".'

'Who said that?' I rasped.

'Your dad. He said once he'd started something he liked to see it through to its conclusion and that he needed Ms P's commitment, one hundred per cent.'

I blinked hard. *Commitment!* This was bad. Seriously bad.

Kaboodle went on, 'Then she said that he was absolutely wonderful and the answer to all her dreams, and he said, "No, no Fenella, it's you who are the wonderful one"—'

'Stop,' I croaked. My hands were clammy.

Kaboodle licked me gently. 'You don't want me to tell you any more?' he asked.

'There's more?' I asked.

'Well, your dad did say, "Fenella, I don't know how to thank you. Meeting you has changed my life. Nothing so exciting has happened to me in years."'

I stared at him in silence. Well, what on earth was there to say?

17

Scenes You Shouldn't See

The next morning, I was up and dressed as soon as the light had crept in around the edges of the curtains.

'Bertie?' Jazz had woken up and was yawning widely and stretching. She looked a bit like a crumpled version of Kaboodle after one of his catnaps, except that her braids were tangled and some had flopped over her face. 'Why are you pacing up and down like that? What's the time?'

'I – I've got to get home, Jazz,' I mumbled, and started stuffing my PJs and things into the bag I'd brought with me.

'Hey, slow down!' Jazz cried, sitting up in bed

and rubbing her eyes. 'I've only just woken up. Don't you want to make breakfast?'

Jazz's parents liked to take things easy most weekends, so Jazz and I were allowed to put ourselves in charge of breakfast and made yummy stuff like pancakes or waffles or bacon and eggs.

'Not hungry,' I said sulkily.

Jazz sighed. 'You still worried about your dad?' she asked, swinging her legs out of bed. She came over and put her arm around me. She smelt warm and sleepy. I put my head on her shoulder and gave a shuddery sigh. 'Hey, don't worry. We'll find out exactly what's going on and then we'll come right out with it and ask your dad about it and tell him you're upset.'

I jerked my head up and stared at her, horrified. 'I can't do that!' I protested. 'I mean, I want to know what's going on, but I really, really do not want to talk to Dad about his love life!'

'I know,' Jazz said soothingly, as though she

was trying to calm a frightened puppy, 'But maybe you'll discover you've got the wrong end of the stick and then you won't have to talk to your dad about anything after all.'

I bristled when she said this. What did *she* know? Dad had talked about *commitment* to Pinkella! He'd said 'nothing this exciting had happened to him for years'! If that didn't mean they were in love, I didn't know what did. But I couldn't tell Jazz any of this. She'd want to know how I knew.

Jazz was right about one thing, though. I did need to find out more, and I needed to find out a way of surprising Dad and Pinkella when they were together so that I could confront them. But Jazz was going to be as much use as a firework in a wheelie bin when it came to spying on Dad. She always got so overexcited and carried away. She wouldn't be able to creep around and act invisible to find out the information we needed.

Only a cat could do that.

Scenes You Shouldn't See

I agreed to make the pancakes anyway, as it was only half past eight, and it was not as though I could achieve much in the way of spying at that time on a Saturday morning.

'You need something to keep your strength up,' Jazz assured me.

So for the next hour or so, I was back to being a normal eleven-year-old, cooking with my best friend, laughing and dancing to the music on the radio, while Tyson made the most of his parents having a lie-in and ate his body-weight in maple syrup – and smeared a load more of it over his face and in his hair. Personally I was on course to set the world record for the amount of chocolate spread to be consumed in one sitting (which kind of showed a fatal flaw in my previous statement that I was 'not hungry').

Eventually, though, the facts had to be faced.

'I've gotta go, Jazz,' I said, as we stacked the

dishwasher and wiped the table. 'Don't forget we've got a ton of homework, which might even possibly be worse than Dad being in love!' I tried to joke, but it came out rather hollow-sounding.

'Wooooo!' Tyson jeered unhelpfully. 'In LURVE!'

'Shut up!' Jazz barked, whacking him professionally on the back of the head. He went off howling to find their mum.

Jazz rolled her eyes at the sound of her little brother wailing and her mum complaining, then she put her head on one side and examined me carefully. 'Listen, don't get too stressy, OK? I've got modern and tap later, but you will come and tell me what's up after, won't you?' She put an arm round me and squeezed me to her.

'Hmm.'

Dad wasn't in when I got back. I ran through the house shouting for him, throwing open all the

258

doors and even checking in the garden, not that Dad goes out there unless he is forced into mowing the lawn because it is about to engulf the house like some hairy, green, house-eating monster.

I was beginning to panic. Dad is never out unless it's something to do with work which he's told me about a million times in advance. In any case, what on earth would require him to do research on a Saturday morning at ten o'clock? Surely even Mrs Moany Miggins and her Sticky-Beak Brigade didn't need interviewing about car parks at that time on a weekend?

I was about to run back to Jazz's when there was a rustle in the leaves above my head and a piti-ful 'mew!'

I looked up. 'Stuck again, are we?' I cried, see-ing Kaboodle balancing precariously on the end of a branch, which was sending showers of autumn-yellow leaves cascading into my hair. 'Hey! Stop jiggling the branch like that!' I protested, shaking

259

my head and brushing the leaves off me. 'My hair's enough of a nightmare without any further foliage decoration, thank you very much.'

'Sorry, I'm sure,' squeaked Kaboodle, his ears flat and his eyes wide with alarm. 'And for your information, I am not stuck —' Sure, you don't look it at all. 'I have been trying to get your attention for the past five minutes, while you have been rustling around the garden like a demented hound on the scent of a rabbit.'

'Charming,' I snorted. 'Why don't you jump down then?'

'All in good time,' said Kaboodle, wobbling even more dangerously and holding on with his claws fully extended as if his life depended on it. 'I have some news for you.'

'Right,' I said, bracing myself. 'Come on then, spit it out.'

Scenes You Shouldn't See

Kaboodle waved his tail tetchily at me and bared his teeth as if he really was going to spit.

'All right, all right! No need to be like that,' I said. 'Here, jump into my arms. I'll catch you – promise.'

Kaboodle put his head on one side as if assessing the situation and then flung himself through the air, his four legs sticking out, coming towards me like a mini black furry kite tumbling out of the sky.

'Ooof!' I caught him with some difficulty as his claws were still out. 'Don't scratch! There, you're OK now,' I soothed, stroking his back once he'd settled himself in my arms.

Kaboodle started purring and washing a paw as if he had not been fearing for his life five seconds earlier, but merely taking an early morning rooftop stroll.

'So,' I said, 'perhaps you could do me a favour now?'

261

Kaboodle stopped washing and looked up at me quizzically. 'Yes?'

I came straight to the point. 'Dad's not here. I'm starting to think he might be at your place.'

'Oh yes,' said Kaboodle carelessly. 'That's what I wanted to tell you. Your dad went over to Ms P's early this morning and they are in the sitting room.'

He wriggled out of my arms, jumped nimbly to the ground and starting trotting off in the direction of the side path that led to the front of the house.

My jaw had dropped to below my knees and someone had superglued my feet to the ground.

Kaboodle glanced over his shoulder at me. 'What are you waiting for? Come on!'

Somehow I managed to communicate to my feet that they should wrench themselves off the grass and move in Kaboodle's direction, but my brain had gone into shut-down mode. I couldn't face thinking about what I was going to see if I followed Kaboodle across the road. Somewhere in the depths of my mind I made a decision to do as the kitten told me, and soon I was sneaking down Pinkella's side path and into her garden.

'Leave this first part to me,' Kaboodle instructed. 'I will go in through the cat flap and act the cute little kitty-cat so as not to arouse suspicion. I'll curl up somewhere near Ms P and your dad so that I can watch and hear everything that is going on. How does that sound?'

I nodded and then hissed, 'Just don't get too comfy, Kaboodle. I don't want you dozing off like you did last time.' I gulped. My stomach was a churning mass of writhing worms and I suddenly wished I hadn't had that last pancake. 'OK – in you go.' I motioned towards the cat flap. 'I'll sit on the bench out here.'

Kaboodle stepped lightly into the house and was gone. I sat down. Then I stood up. I wished I'd brought a book or something. I wished I'd brought Jazz. I wished I hadn't agreed to follow Kaboodle here at all.

I paced around the garden, counting each step to try and distract myself. I glanced at my watch. Kaboodle had only been in there five minutes. What if he had to stay in there for half an hour until he found out anything useful?

I didn't think I could hang around any longer. It was doing my head in. I was just about to stomp off home and wait for Dad to eventually come back, when Kaboodle hurtled through the cat flap as though someone had just set his tail alight.

'I think you should come – NOW!' he insisted.

'Whoa! Hold on a minute!' I shouted, holding a hand up to stop him. 'You've got to tell me what's going on first – I'm not charging into Ms P's un-invited only to discover her and Dad . . . well, her and Dad doing what exactly?' I finished queasily.

Kaboodle was washing his chest furiously and

refusing to meet my eye. Risking being scratched into oblivion, I scooped him up, catching him unawares. Cupping his little heart-shaped face in my free hand I said, 'Tell – me – Kaboodle.'

'Oh dear,' he mewed.

I waited, holding on to him as tightly as I could.

Kaboodle wriggled slightly, but gave up when it was obvious he wasn't going anywhere without me. 'OK, OK!' he squealed finally. 'But let go of me, can't you?' I did as he asked and he shook himself irritably. 'Follow me.'

Kaboodle headed into the house and made his way to the kitchen. I tried to follow in a calm and collected manner, but inside my head I was screaming, 'Let me at 'em!'

We appeared in the doorway of the living room in time to see my Dad on one knee, gazing adoringly at Pinkella while she gushed, 'Oh my darling man! You are the answer to all my dreams!'

And Dad replied, 'No, no, Fenella — it's you who has made this so perfect.'

A strangled exclamation halfway between a shriek and a sob escaped from my mouth and Dad tore his eyes away from Fenella to see me standing there, my jaw hanging open, my hands limp at my sides.

'Bertie!' he cried.

I turned and ran back out the way I had come, nearly stamping on Kaboodle in the process and causing him to yowl in fright. I didn't care though. I didn't care about anything other than getting away from the appalling scene I had just witnessed.

Dad had asked Pinkella to marry him, and she had just accepted.

Pinkella was going to be my new mum.

18
Out in the Cold

I kept on running until I reached the park where I sat down on a bench and cried and cried and cried.

A few days ago, my only worry had been Kaboodle trying to make off with Houdini and Mr Nibbles as meals on wheels. Now Kaboodle's owner was the one trying to make off with something: my dad. And it was pretty obvious where this left me – out in the cold. No wonder that Pink Permutation had sucked up to me so much and asked me to look after her beloved pussy-wussy-catkins. She'd had her eye on Dad all along. She had used me to get to him. She had—

267

Kitten Kaboodle

'Berrrrrtie?'

It was Kaboodle, purring like a hairdryer on overdrive and winding his way round my legs.

'Go away!' I shouted.

A passing man walking his dog gave me a funny look and then walked quickly in the other direction.

'I'm sorry,' Kaboodle said softly.

I sighed a wobbly, tear-filled sigh and scooped Kaboodle up into my arms without waiting for an invitation. I knew none of this was his fault. I couldn't speak, though – couldn't tell him what was going on in my mind. I was so confused. I ended up burying my face in his fur and breathing in that dark musky smell of his.

Kaboodle purred an even deeper purr and licked my cheek with his sandpaper tongue. We sat there, saying nothing, until I began to feel hungry.

268

Out in the Cold

I didn't want to go home though, and I didn't have any money. I got up and motioned for Kaboodle to follow me. I needed to move around to stop myself from freezing solid.

We walked through the park. We must have looked odd, a girl taking a kitten for a walk, but my mind was on other things.

'What am I going to do?' I asked Kaboodle at last. I flumped down on to another bench and settled Kaboodle back on to my lap and stroked him, as much to keep myself warm as to pet him.

'You know, Bertie, one good thing could come out of all this,' Kaboodle said.

'Oh yeah?' I snapped. He wasn't going to try and convince me that Pinkella would be a good mum, like Jazz had the night before, was he?

'Well, if your dad marries Ms P, you and I will be living together,' Kaboodle purred.

I nodded quietly. That would be cool. But it didn't make me change my mind.

269

'Let's go to Jazz's,' Kaboodle suggested, breaking the silence.

I must have looked surprised at this suggestion, because Kaboodle put his head on one side and fixed me with a serious look. 'I hate to admit it but she's going to be more help to you than I can ever be,' he added sadly. 'I can't exactly offer you a place to stay or give you any food, can I?'

He was right. All I wanted right that minute was for my best friend to give me a hug and tell me everything was going to be OK. Minutes later I plodded up the driveway to Jazz's front door, shivering quite violently now, rubbing my arms and stomping my feet to keep warm. Kaboodle sat by me while we waited for someone to come to the door.

'Shouldn't you go home?' I muttered through chattering teeth.

270

Out in the Cold

'No,' he said simply. 'I'm not leaving you until I know you'll be all right.'

A light flicked on in the hall and there was the sound of running footsteps, then Jazz flung open the front door.

'Thank goodness!' she screamed and flung her arms round me, whipping my face with her braids. 'We were so worried.'

'Eh?' I mumbled into a mouthful of hair and beads. What was Jazz worried about? She didn't know I'd run off—

'Bertie!'

I backed out of Jazz's arms sharply. I was face to face with Dad.

'No!' I cried. 'I don't want to talk to you! I don't want to see you ever again!'

I turned back to the door but Jazz had placed herself firmly in front of it and wouldn't let me out. Dad came up behind me and put his hands on my shoulders.

'You're freezing!' he said, trying to hug me.

I whirled round and pummelled my fists at him. 'Get off me!' I yelled. 'Get off! Go and find your *girlfriend* and get her to give you a hug.'

'My WHAT?' Dad cried.

'I tried to tell you, Mr F,' said Jazz.

He caught hold of my elbows and shook me gently. 'Bertie, what girlfriend?' he asked, his voice struggling to hide an urgent tone.

'Oh, please. You know exactly what girl-friend!' I spat. 'Pinkella – I mean, *Fen*-ella – Ms PINKINGTON!' I yelled.

'Told you,' said Jazz.

And then Dad did something completely unexpected, and in the circumstances, totally unset-tling.

He laughed.

And it wasn't just a snort or a chortle. It was a full-on, throat-wobbling, belly-exploding, out-of-control eruption that filled the hallway and shook

272

me to my boots. Or trainers. He let go of my elbows and held his own sides as he fought to get his breath back.

I stood there, glowering at him, hands on hips, waiting for this bout of hysteria to stop. Jazz shrugged and pulled a face as if to say, 'No idea what that's all about.'

I tapped my foot impatiently.

Kaboodle, meanwhile, had gone into hiding under the coat stand and whispered, 'I think you should phone for the vet. He looks as if he needs to be put out of his misery.'

I shot a withering look in his direction and then shouted above the ridiculous cacophony of whooping and wheezing gathering force in front of me, 'WILL SOMEONE PLEASE TELL ME WHAT IS SO AMUSING?'

Dad wiped his eyes extravagantly on the back of his sleeve and motioned for me to follow him.

In the kitchen he pulled up a couple of chairs,

273

and still wheezing and hiccuping with the remnants of hysteria, he made it clear he wanted me to sit down. I did, but I was frowning hard and feeling very confused, not to say hurt. Jazz had followed at a safe distance and stood in the doorway. Her mum appeared over her shoulder and looked as though she was about to ask what was going on, but the expression on my face probably changed her mind. In any case, she disappeared swiftly, whispering to Jazz and dragging her away by the arm.

Dad reached across the table and took one of my hands. I tried to pull it away, but he held on firmly. 'Listen, Bertie,' he said, in a suddenly serious tone that forced me to look him in the eye, 'I am not going out with Fenella Pinkington, OK?' He waited for my reaction. I didn't satisfy him with one. 'I'm not going out with *anyone*! Bertie, you've got to believe me! Whatever gave you that idea?'

That's when I really exploded. 'OH, I've absolutely NO IDEA what could have given me the

impression that you and that PINK PERSON were dating!' I yelled. 'Now, let me see . . . could it be that you went out with her last night and shoved me over here to get me out of the way? Or that you've spent more time with her these past two days than you've spent with me in the past year? Or that I walked in on you today while you were DOWN ON ONE KNEE AND DECLARING YOUR UNDYING LOVE FOR THE WOMAN?' I ended, narrowing my eyes at him witheringly.

I was pleased to see that Dad's jaw had dropped so low that it was practically lying on the floor. And the temperature in the room seemed to have dropped a few degrees.

The only sound was the fridge humming like a demented wasp.

Eventually Dad closed his mouth. He made a throat-clearing sound and a look of bewilderment crossed his face. 'Bertie,' he said finally, and I hardly recognized his voice, it was so small and hurt, 'how could you think those things? I'm so sorry.' He shook his head. 'I owe you an explanation.'

I nodded a bit shakily, my lips firmly clamped in a tight line, quivering with anticipation and fear. Somewhere deep inside I knew I was being a bit dramatic, but I didn't care.

Dad blinked, took off his glasses and cleaned them on his shirt. 'Bertie,' he said slowly, 'I've been working on something for a while. A private writing project. I hadn't told anyone about it because it was just a bit of a dream, really. Pie in the sky. A kind of release from the rubbish I have to write for my job. I never imagined I would actually show it to anyone. But then I got chatting to Fenella last weekend when she came home early from her, erm, unfortunate experience in Scotland.'

He stopped and looked at me.

'So?'

Dad took a deep breath and continued. 'OK, let me start from the beginning,' he said.

19
The Play's the Thing

Dad cleared his throat and shuffled in his chair. I bit my nails nervously. Then he began.

'Remember Fenella said she'd gone for an audition for a film called *Love, Don't You Know?*' he asked, 'and she'd been rejected because the director said she was too old for a leading role in a romantic comedy? Well, we were chatting about this and how awful and ageist it was, and then Fenella asked me what I did for a living and so I told her about my dreary job.'

'What has this got to do with anything?' I muttered, getting impatient again.

Dad smiled weakly. 'I was just getting to that,'

he said. 'I was sympathizing with Fenella about the fact that it gets harder and harder to find interesting jobs once you're older, and that it was the younger writers on the newspaper who are picked to cover the best stories. Then suddenly Fenella had a brainwave.'

'Good grief!' I muttered. 'Was it pink, by any chance?'

Dad raised his eyebrows and said, 'She suggested that I have a go at writing something for her.'

'What, an article about being "In the Pink"?' I jeered.

'No,' said Dad, completely ignoring my sarcasm. 'A play!' His eyes twinkled.

'A play,' I repeated, putting my hands on my hips.

'Yes!' said Dad. 'So I said, "Well, it's funny you should say that because I've been writing a play for months in my spare time," and she said, "How thrilling!" and asked if she could read it.' Dad

paused as if he was waiting for me to say something, but when it became obvious that I wasn't going to, he finished, 'So that's what we've been doing together.'

I still didn't completely understand. 'What do you mean? WHAT have you been doing together?'

'Working on the script!' Dad beamed. 'Fenella took the first draft away with her last weekend and asked if we could meet up again last night. She said she would give me some feedback and promised to be brutally honest. I was so worried that she would think it was a load of nonsense that I didn't want to tell you about it until she had read it, so I kept it a secret from you.'

'Well, thanks a lot, Dad,' I said. 'You had a right go at me when I didn't tell you about the Pet-Sitting Service, and then you go and keep a secret like this from me? *And* let me go around believing you and . . . that woman were going on a date!'

Dad blushed. 'I know. I'm sorry.' He looked down at the table and began tracing patterns on the wipe-clean tablecloth, like a child being told off by the teacher.

Poor Dad. He was so excited about this play thing. He just wanted me to be excited about it too.

I came round to his side of the table and put my arms around him and leaned my head on his shoulder.

'I really am sorry, Bertie,' he mumbled. 'I'm a rubbish dad, I know – working all the time, palming you off on Jazz and her family. I just find it so hard sometimes, keeping things going and doing that stupid, boring old job just to pay the bills. I've tried to do my best, y'know,' he added softly.

I pulled away from him and hoicked myself up on to the table to face him. He looked up at me and smiled faintly. 'Tell me about this play, then,' I said, smiling encouragingly.

280

The Play's the Thing

Dad's face brightened and he said, 'Really? You want to know?'

I nodded.

And then he told me that he'd had an idea about a year ago to write a play which was a romantic comedy, and he'd started on it in the evenings when I'd gone to bed. It had become a bit of an obsession though, and soon he found himself wanting to write it at weekends too. He was struggling to meet his deadlines for the newspaper as well as scribbling at his play, which was why he'd been so away-with-the-fairies most of the time.

'Anyway, the great thing is that Fenella loves the idea!' he explained. 'And she thinks that with her contacts in the theatre and film industries and with my local contacts through the paper, we could put on our own production of it, right here in town! And on top of that, she thinks this could be just the thing to save the old theatre that everyone's got so heated about.'

'What – the one that's going to be knocked down and turned into a car park?' I asked.

'Yes,' said Dad. 'That'll shut the old moaning minnies up – and it'll make a much better story for the local paper too.'

Something had just occurred to me. 'But if Fenella's too old to get a part in the film she was auditioning for, won't she be too old to star in a play?'

'You're forgetting how much people love it when a celebrity does something local! And anyway, my play is written specifically for the "more mature leading lady",' said Dad. I rolled my eyes at the dramatic tone in his voice. 'It's tailor-made for the older actress. Fenella says it's got everything: humour, pathos, romance. She thinks it could be a hit!'

I rolled my eyes even more. As if Dad was going to be the next best thing in Hollywood since plastic surgery!

The Play's the Thing

'So you're definitely not going out with her?' I asked, just double-checking.

'Come here, you noodle,' he said. 'There's room for only one real leading lady in my life.' Dad smiled and opened his arms. It was a bit of an awkward hug with me still perched on the table, but it was a lovely one all the same.

'Ahem!'

I peered over Dad's shoulder to see Jazz had reappeared, and was holding a disgruntled-looking Kaboodle.

'When you two have finished all that soppy making-up stuff,' said Jazz, 'I thought you'd like to see who I found skulking in the hallway.' She held Kaboodle out to me as if he were a parcel of sausages.

'I was not skulking,' said Kaboodle, through gritted teeth. His ears were so flat in indignation that I could hardly make them out. 'I was trying to find a way out of this overheated hellhole. I could tell that I wasn't wanted any more. And besides,' he sniffed, 'I needed the loo.'

'Oh no! I hope you didn't have an accident!' I cried, and then gasped, my hand flying to cover my mouth.

Jazz was frowning at me with her you're-a-nutcase look again. It was becoming a bit too regular an occurrence, her looking at me like that.

'What's going on?' said Dad. 'Who's had an accident?'

'No one,' said Kaboodle. 'We felines are far too hygienic to embarrass ourselves in that way.'

'Good,' I whispered.

Jazz sighed. 'Like I said, now you and your dad are mates again, can you take this cat off me? He must have followed you here. I think you should take him back to Ms P's.'

Dad said, 'Oh, is that Fenella's kitten? Strudel or something?'

The Play's the Thing

'*Kaboodle*,' Jazz and I chorused.

'Obadiah de la Chasse, actually,' said Kaboodle. 'But, oh, what's the point?'

I giggled. 'Yeah, we'll take him home,' I said, jumping down off the table and letting Jazz put the little cat into my arms.

'I'll come with you,' said Dad, putting an arm around my shoulders. 'Fenella and I can tell you a bit more about the play, then.'

'Play?' said Jazz. 'What play?'

'Oh yeah, Dad's been writing—'

'Nothing,' said Dad hastily, gripping my shoulder a bit too tightly.

'Da-ad?' I said, looking up at him.

'I – I'm not ready to tell everyone about it yet,' he said.

'Dad, you know what? I think we've got to make a pact,' I said firmly.

'Oh yes? What's that then?' Dad asked, looking worried.

'We've got to promise not to keep any more secrets,' I said. 'I kept the pet-sitting from you, and that was wrong, I admit it. But you should have told me what you and Ms P were up to, and not left me to put two and two together and make one hundred and fifty-six!'

'You're right,' said Dad. He took a deep breath and looking at Jazz said, 'I've written a play and Fenella reckons it's quite good, so we're hoping to do a production of it in the old town theatre.'

'Yay!' said Jazz, jumping up and down and clapping her hands. 'Can I be in it? I'll do anything – I'll even be backstage if you like.'

Dad laughed. 'We'll see,' he said.

'Just as long as you keep me out of it,' hissed Kaboodle.

I grinned. 'No worries,' I whispered in one tiny ear.

'And, Bertie,' Dad added, giving my shoulder a squeeze, 'you do realize how bonkers you've been,

don't you?' he laughed. 'Honestly! Can you imagine me and Fenella – a couple?'

Kaboodle stretched and flexed his front claws.
'Not really,' he said.

I shook my head at the little kitten. 'Your
miaow is sharper than your claws, you know,' I
breathed.

Kaboodle nuzzled my cheek and purred.

EPILOGUE
A Twist in the Tail

Life was Full Steam Ahead after that. Pinkella was in the paper nearly every other day, promoting the refurbishment of the old theatre and giving loads of interviews about the play. She got hordes of her old thespian 'luvvies' to pledge their money to the upkeep of the theatre and ran a campaign called 'Keep Theatre Alive and Kicking!'

And then, once the theatre was up and running, rehearsals started in earnest for Dad's play, *Love for Old Time's Sake*.

The opening night got such fantastic reviews that the rest of the run was a sell-out and Dad was soon hounded with calls from actors and directors

alike, asking him to write more plays. It was, as he could not stop telling me, his 'dream come true', especially as it meant he could finally quit his boring old job on the *Daily Ranter*.

And it was pretty cool for me, as it meant he worked from home all the time and didn't have to go out investigating stupid car park stories. We got to spend loads more time together.

We also spent quite a lot more time with Pinkella. But that was fine by me now I knew she wasn't plotting to take Dad away. And I finally had to admit that she actually was quite a nice person once I got to know her properly. Especially when Dad took her aside one day and put her straight about calling me Roberta and fussing over my hair and she actually apologized to me!

Pinkella's career had taken on a new lease of life after the success of the play. She had been the star of the show, and received letters by the bucketful every day from directors who wanted to put her in other plays and films.

'And it's all thanks to you, Bertie dear,' she told me. 'If it hadn't been for your Pet-Sitting Service, I would never have come round that night after those dreadful auditions and I would never have had that chat with your wonderful father. You have changed everything for the better, Bertie! You are an angel.'

She was so grateful, she asked me and Jazz to look after Kaboodle on a regular basis while the play was on, and she paid us a fiver a day – 'Result!' as Jazz put it. She could have bought *ten* pairs of those trainers she'd wanted by the time the curtain dropped on the last performance!

But then suddenly it was all over.

Pinkella told us she was moving.

'I'm so sorry,' she said, taking in the looks of surprise and shock on our faces. 'I just can't live so

glaringly in the public eye any more, darlings,' she said. 'I need to get away from it all. And besides, I'm going to be on the road so much with all the new work I'm getting.'

'We'll miss you,' said Dad, blushing. He was never very good at saying stuff like that.

'And Kaboodle,' I said, swallowing hard.

'Yes, darling, and we'll miss you too,' said Pinkella. 'We'll come and visit you from time to time though. And of course you must come and see us.'

Dad took her through to the kitchen to make a cup of tea and I sat down on the sofa, my head in my hands. What would I do without Kaboodle? He'd become as good a friend to me as Jazz. He was almost as much my pet as Pinkella's. Life was going to be so empty without him around. My brain was whizzing around in overdrive, and I was so preoccupied, I almost missed the tiny mewling noise coming from outside the front door.

I went to the window and peered out on to the drive.

'Kaboodle!' I cried and ran to open the door.

He trotted up to the porch and said, 'Mffuuggggle.'

I stared in horror as I realized there was a small bundle of fur hanging from his jaws. 'Oh no, it's not a . . . a *mouse*?' I asked shakily.

'Of course not!' Kaboodle protested, dropping his offering.

Only then did I get a proper look at what he had been carrying.

'A kitten?' I squealed.

'Full marks for observation,' Kaboodle said coolly. 'I thought you might like her.'

'She's — she's *for me*?' I asked, hardly daring to go anywhere near the tiny creature, which wasn't much larger than the palm of my hand. 'But where did you get her?' She was orange and white. A tiny

A Twist in the Tail

stripy marmalade cat, with the largest crystal blue eyes I'd ever seen.

Kaboodle gave a rasping sound as

if he was clearing his throat. 'I – er – let's just say she needs a loving home,' he said cryptically. 'Best not to ask too many questions. I thought you might like a farewell gift. You'll have heard by now that we're leaving?'

'Oh, Kaboodle, thank you. She's gorgeous! What's her name?'

'Well, her mother called her Perdita de la Chasse—' he began.

'De la Chasse?' I asked. 'But isn't that your—?'

'Anyway, feel free to call her whatever you like. You humans normally do,' cut in Kaboodle. He washed a front paw earnestly and then, as if to make it clear that this conversation was over, he turned, holding his tail high in the air, and called out over one shoulder, 'I thought it was about time you had your own cat. Especially now I won't be around for much longer. And I think you'll make a lovely companion for the little one.'

That was the closest Kaboodle had ever come to paying me a compliment, I realized, as I bent down to scoop up the tiny kitten. I watched as the black and white cat who had been my friend for the past year trotted back over to Pinkella's. I wanted to call out something, but my throat had closed up. He gave his tail a final flick in my direction as he disappeared down the side of the house.

What on earth will Dad say? I thought, as I slowly turned to go inside.

'Oh, look at that adorable little baby!'

It was Pinkella, who'd just come out of the kitchen with two coffee mugs in her hands.

Dad came after her. 'Oh good grief, what's that?' he cried. 'It's not another blinking mouse, is it?'

Pinkella smiled at him as if he were a rather foolish small child and said, 'Marvin, darling, it's a gorgeous little kitten!'

I just stood there, holding the kitten and looking up at Dad with what I hoped were the hugest, most pleading, I'm-your-only-daughter-and-you-owe-me-big-time eyes.

Dad looked at Pinkella, and Pinkella looked at Dad. Then he turned to me, sighed, and said, 'So what are you going to call her?'

A Message from the Author

When I was younger I used to be just like Bertie: totally and utterly petless and desperate to do something about it. I didn't come up with anything as ingenious as a pet-sitting service though. No, I just nagged and pestered my mum and dad. Over and over and over again. As you can imagine, this did not get me very far! I ended up with some stick insects, which I got from school. We had been observing them for a nature project and were allowed to keep a few for ourselves in a jam jar. For some unknown reason I was not very popular when I brought them home with me . . . Anyway, they died eventually and I persuaded mum and dad to let me have a tortoise. But sadly the tortoise died too, and so I was back to square one . . .

Then (oh happy day!) my friend Helen announced that her cat had had kittens! I pleaded with mum to 'just come and look' at the kittens, and that was when Inky entered our lives. We adored her and all her crazy habits, from the way she would sit on the windowsill and hurl insults at the birds outside to the way she would use the sugar bowl as an emergency loo. (OK, that only happened once, but she'll always be remembered for it!) She was the one who taught me that cats are trying to tell us things all the time, if only we will listen properly. I quickly learned to understand when Inky wanted food or cuddles, or a warm place to curl up and sleep.

Many years later, I started dropping hints to my husband about how lovely it would be to have a cat in our home. He was (and still is) Definitely Not a Cat Person, so you can imagine his response. But all was not lost – I remembered my old trick, and asked if I could 'just go and look' at two RSPCA rescue kittens . . . and what do you know? Jet and Inky Mark II have been with us now for five years! Inky Mark II reminds me a lot of the original Inky, except that she hurls insults at me instead of the birds and is prone to turning her back and sulking if I don't feed her the minute she demands it. She has also been known to launch raids on the larder if she has completely run out of patience. Jet is more mild-mannered and loves people. So much so that she found herself a second home last year – but that's another story, and one which inspired my next book, KITTEN SMITTEN.

Both cats have had to come to terms with sharing their lives with Kenna the Pooch, who was the inspiration for PUPPY LOVE and the other books in that series. When she first came to live with us Kenna was the same size and colour (black) as Inky and Jet. I could just see her thinking, 'Goody! Two little pups just like me!' She would try to play with them, but they were never interested and made their feelings clear by hissing and scratching! Now Kenna is five times bigger than the cats so they don't bother with the hissing and scratching and instead reluctantly put up with being licked and nuzzled by our soppy pooch.

Life certainly is pretty crazy when you get to share it with animals, but I wouldn't have it any other way! Do you have pets that do crazy things or are just plain cute? If so, I'd love to hear from you! Write to me at:

Anna Wilson
c/o Macmillan Children's Books
20 New Wharf Road
London N1 9RR
United Kingdom

Love,
Anna
xxx

Moira Munro, the illustrator of this book, is pitifully allergic to furry animals. It is a Terrible Tragedy not to have a pet to stroke, and it can drive one quite loopy. This is why there is probably not a single story or picture by Moira Munro that doesn't feature some kind of cuddly creature. Luckily Moira Munro does have a daughter, (called Chloe) who is at least as cuddly as a kitten. Chloe is also very useful as she can draw the cutest cat ever – for a year's pocket money. She did the one in the 'Order of Service' written by Jazz on page 95.